B.C.

Distracted, Derrick almost missed the two police cars heading for the barn.

And the television news van that followed.

Quickly, he dismounted the horse, handed the reins over to the evening stable hand and dashed to Emilie's office. But already two policemen were escorting her through the front doors of the stable. One of the officers held up a hand, indicating for Derrick to stay back.

Emilie lowered her head and looked away. "Call my lawyer. And my father."

"And tell them what?" Derrick's voice cracked through the tense air.

"Can't you guess? I'm being arrested," she said, trying to sound bravely unaffected.

Derrick could see she was close to tears. "For what?"

"For the murder of Camillo Garcia," one of the officers answered.

Books by Kit Wilkinson

Love Inspired Suspense

Protector's Honor
Sabotage

KIT WILKINSON

is a former Ph.D. student who once wrote discussions on the medieval feminine voice. She now prefers weaving stories of romance and redemption. Her first inspirational manuscript won the prestigious RWA Golden Heart and was published in 2009 by Steeple Hill Books as *Protector's Honor.* Besides writing, she loves hanging out with friends and family, cooking for lots of people and participating in almost any sport. She and her husband reside in Virginia with their two young children and one extremely energetic border collie mix named Bear.

SABOTAGE

Kit Wilkinson

Steeple
Hill®

Published by Steeple Hill Books™

STEEPLE HILL BOOKS

Steeple
Hill®

Recycling programs
for this product may
not exist in your area.

ISBN-13: 978-0-373-67420-6

SABOTAGE

Copyright © 2010 by Kit Wilkinson

www.SteepleHill.com

Printed in U.S.A.

Some trust in chariots and some in horses,
but we trust in the name of the Lord our God.
—*Psalms* 20:7

To the real Emilie Ann, may your life be filled with love and the blessing of the Lord

PROLOGUE

*B*urn it.

Camillo Garcia tossed the logbook into a metal can and struck a match. Holding the tiny blaze in front of him, he watched the hungry flame eat its way up the stem.

Confess your sins to each other. The words of scripture swept through his head like a whisper, gripped his lungs and constricted his airways. The little flame reached his fingertips and he dropped the match to the concrete floor and snuffed it out with his boot.

He couldn't destroy the evidence.

But hide it?

Maybe *that* would buy him the time he needed.

Camillo spun around and faced the stall of the most valuable horse in the stable.

Perfect.

He stepped inside and gave the stallion a pat. Then, using a hoof pick, he pried a section of paneling from the front corner. The plank bent away just enough to drop the logbook inside the wall. Camillo took a letter from his pocket and placed it between the pages, then he slipped the logbook between the studs and allowed the sheet of paneling to snap back into position.

Satisfied, he hurried back to his office at a nervous pace. Leaning over his desk, he composed another note. The pen trembled in his hand as he struggled for the right words. They didn't come, so he wrote what he could. When he finished, he centered the paper on his desk and placed his keys next to it.

With one last look around, he slung the strap of his duffel bag over his shoulder and hurried through the facility—the state-of-the-art stable where he'd worked as groom and exerciser for four years. Regret and shame slowed his steps. Despite the cold, Camillo wiped heavy beads of sweat from his brow. He thought of his mother and younger brothers in Mexico, dependent on his income. He didn't want to leave. He had to. And he had no one to blame for that but himself.

A hoof clapped against a stall and echoed through the quiet stable. The sharp sound urged him on, helping to slough away his heavy emotions. Camillo exited the stable and set out down a dark path between the fields. Then, cutting through the woods, he reached the edge of the estate. From there, the station would be an hour's walk. Then three days on a bus to California. He prayed he would make it.

Bits of asphalt crunched under his feet as he

walked along the highway stretched before him like an abyss. He walked on until a pair of headlights illuminated the ground around him. Panic prickled through him. His heart thumped against his chest. He stopped and turned into the bright lights. The car rolled to a stop beside him. Its fancy engine purred low. The passenger in the back waved a pistol at his chest. The driver ordered him to get in.

He slid into the familiar car, knowing why they'd come. It was for the logbook. Camillo prayed for his mother as the cold metal of the gun pressed into his neck and the car accelerated into the night.

ONE

Emilie Gill struggled to concentrate, but keeping her mind on riding and off of Camillo had proven impossible. Even with a renowned trainer evaluating her performance, she couldn't focus. And his disapproval might cost her a spot on the Olympic team. Still, it couldn't be helped. Something had happened to her groom. Something bad. She could sense it in her bones.

Emilie tried to shake away the distressing thoughts. Clenching the double reins, she sunk her weight into the heels of her tall black boots and coaxed the young mare onward to begin the course of fences.

The approach. Her braid struck down between her shoulders, marking the number of strides to the fence. *One... Two... Three...*

Takeoff. Together they soared over the four-foot spread of boxwoods and rails. Her hands and torso moved above the horse's arched neck.

Landing. Her weight shifted back to her seat and heels, and beneath, the bay-colored mare gripped the earth.

Emilie turned to the next jump. Eyes up. Always up. Always ahead.

Continuing through the course with the same precision, she and Chelsea completed ten jumps with no faults—but her performance was lackluster. No doubt Mr. Winslow had noticed as well. She shot a furtive glance at the world-renowned trainer sitting nearby in the open stands, his expression indifferent. Emilie swallowed hard then scanned the arena for Camillo. A four-year-old habit was hard to break. She slumped in the saddle and sighed. When would she get it into her thick skull that her once faithful groom, also her best friend, had left? Without any warning. Well, that wasn't exactly true. Camillo had acted a bit strangely over the last few weeks. But when Emilie had asked him what was on his mind, he had said he was just tired. So, she had let it go. And now he'd left with no explanation. Gone.

A light rain began to trickle down. Cold November air whipped through the hilltop space, chafing her exposed cheeks. She steered the mare across the wide arena, hurrying toward the stable.

"Miss Gill, where are you off to?" The severe British accent echoed over the grassy arena. "You cannot retire on that performance. It's simply unacceptable."

Emilie pulled on the reins, trying to erase her frown. Chelsea turned toward the covered portion of the stands where Mr. Winslow had relocated to avoid the drizzle. The older gentleman sat down, lips pursed, with his Burberry raincoat buttoned to the neck and his iPhone pressed to one ear. As she approached, he lowered the phone to his lap and leaned over the edge of the railing.

"Miss Gill, despite your size, your equitation skills are utterly lacking in finesse. I'm sorry to be so blunt, but I'm not a man to mince words. I'd like to see you take this lovely mare 'round again. But with big releases and less cattle driving between the fences. Mr. Randall is lowering the rails for you." He turned away, putting the phone back to his ear.

Emilie lifted her head high and stared at nothing for a long moment, blinking her eyelids against the increasing rainfall.

Mr. Randall?

A deep frown gripped her mouth. Searching the grass ring, her eyes narrowed on a man's figure in full rain gear, lowering jumps in the far corner of the arena. Camillo's replacement. A friend of her sister's who she'd hired over the phone the day before. He'd been scheduled to start that morning. But hadn't bothered to show. Emilie had all but given up on him.

"Did you hear me, Miss Gill? Big releases," the trainer repeated.

She turned back to Mr. Winslow. "Uh. Yes, sir. I was just concerned about pacing."

"Your speed is adequate."

Emilie slumped further into the saddle. His sharp tone crushed her hopes of his ever intending to work with her. Why had he even bothered asking her to ride the course again? What was the point? If only Camillo had been there, he would have known what to say to make her feel right again. Instead, everything was wrong. Everything seemed hopeless.

Emilie pressed her lips together and gathered her wits before heading toward the new hire. And before she did something embarrassing, like cry, in front of Mr. Winslow.

Derrick Randall rushed from one jump to the next, keeping his hood low to fight the cold drizzle. The rider trotted toward him.

"Mr. Randall?" She slowed the horse and walked a tight circle around the fence he was lowering.

Mr. Randall? Derrick lifted an eyebrow as he placed the last rail in the cups.

"It's just Derrick." He stepped toward her and lifted a hand. "Sorry I'm late. Traffic accident."

"You had an accident?" She halted the mare, but made no eye contact, nor did she take his hand. Her pale face was tight. Her jaw clenched. But even angry or anxious or whatever her foul mood, Derrick choked on his breath as he looked at her.

Emilie Gill was one beautiful woman—stunning, actually. She had luminous green eyes, creamy white skin and hair that fell in a long, golden braid. Undone, it might have reached her waist. Her lips were soft and peach-colored under a small, perky nose. Everything arranged for the complete benefit of the viewer.

"I—uh—I wasn't in an accident. Just stuck behind one." Derrick took a deep breath and disregarded her unfriendly greeting. He could hardly blame her for being miffed about his tardiness. His outstretched hand moved to the neck of the gorgeous mare. Her wet coat felt warm against his palm. "She's beautiful. A Warmblood, right? You can always tell breeds by the head and feet."

Emilie's face softened. Finally, she looked down at him. "Yes. She's my latest acquisition. Just arrived from Ireland. They call her Chelsea's Danger."

"Very powerful and yet elegant." Derrick smiled. "And Peter, he's the best. I didn't know you trained with him."

"You know Mr. Winslow?" Astonishment filled her voice.

"Just my whole life." He laughed. "He and my uncle are close friends."

She glanced at Peter in the stands and then looked back, like she couldn't believe the old man had a friend. "Well, he's not my trainer. Not yet, that is."

She turned away in a whirl. Derrick liked the color her strange frustration had added to those creamy cheeks. He hoped she'd get over her anger or anxiety and decide to keep him on. He needed the money if he ever hoped to finish veterinary school. And he wouldn't mind seeing what Miss Emilie Gill looked like when she *wasn't* scowling.

He made his way back to Peter, looking up at the cloudy sky.

Lord, this is all in Your hands…

Guilt nipped at Emilie for not shaking the man's hand. But that gesture would have meant she'd accepted him as her employee and she wasn't sure she wanted to do that. Not even if he was a friend of Mr. Winslow and of her sister. He didn't look anything like a groom. For one, he was huge—more like a football player than a horseman.

And it just seemed wrong, giving Camillo's job to a stranger.

Camillo. Where are you?

Again, this nagging idea that he was in trouble and needed her help overwhelmed her. Only something terribly important would have made him leave without talking to her first. Or something just plain terrible… Why did she have the feeling it was the latter?

Taking a deep breath, she expelled the anxious thoughts and filled her mind with fences and rhythm. She gave Chelsea a quick tap with her heel. Over the course, she executed the big rein releases Mr. Winslow had suggested. They felt awkward. And little by little, doubtful thoughts clouded her focus again. Over the final two jumps, old habits took over. She tightened her stance and Chelsea knocked rails on both fences. Emilie grimaced as the wooden bars thudded to the earth.

Ready to face her criticism and dismissal, she slowed Chelsea and turned toward the covered stand. Mr. Winslow, however, appeared engrossed in conversation with the new hire. Had the trainer not even been watching?

At that moment, Emilie realized she didn't care. Until she heard from Camillo and knew he was safe, she might as well face the fact that she wouldn't be able to concentrate or compete.

As she approached the stands, Mr. Randall jumped to his feet. He took the reins over Chelsea's head with one hand and with the other helped her down from the saddle. Before she could protest, her feet hit the ground and he'd tossed his jacket over the saddle, protecting it from the rain.

"Nice to see you, Peter," Derrick called over his shoulder as he jogged Chelsea back to the barn.

Emilie stepped under the covering. "You were right. Bigger releases. Thank you for coming." Expecting Mr. Winslow to leave, she held out her hand.

"Humph." The trainer waved her arm away. "I'm not quite decided. I want to observe you again and see how you respond to more adjustments. How about I return on Tuesday? Have the Warmblood and the stallion ready." He stood and placed a crumpled hat on his shock of white hair. "Good day, Miss Gill."

Emilie stood openmouthed as the old man left the stands and tromped the short distance to his Range Rover. What was that? Was he still considering her?

Her heart pounded against her chest and she struggled to conceal the smile that wanted to win over her mouth. Forgetting the rain, she moved out from the covered stand and headed toward the barn.

"And Randall is a fine choice," Mr. Winslow shouted from the open window of his SUV.

Emilie landed her foot in a puddle.

"You'll have a hard time finding anyone else with his experience," he added. "I certainly hope you will keep him on."

Emilie searched the old man's face. Wasn't that *her* decision? Cold water seeped through to her toes before she nodded in agreement.

"Until Tuesday." He rolled up his window then sped down the gravel drive.

Emilie shivered, hugging her shoulders as she ran the last few yards to the stable.

"Mr. Randall?" His name echoed through the barn, creating unnatural reverberations that chilled her head to toe. Goose bumps prickled her skin as she removed her helmet and wrung out her wet braid. The brief joy from Mr. Winslow's approval had already gone, replaced with the same dread that had haunted her since finding Camillo's note.

She grabbed a thick wool blanket from the top of a tack trunk, draped it over her shoulders then crossed the spacious foyer to check the thermostat.

"Wow, you are one tiny rider." A deep baritone sounded from behind.

Emilie muffled a squeal, dropping one end of the blanket.

"Did I startle you?" Derrick's accent, maybe Tennessee, seemed heavier than it had over the phone. "Sorry about that."

Emilie shook her head but remained facing the wall as she adjusted the temperature a few degrees. Heat crept up her spine as she could feel Derrick's eyes on her back. She turned. "I'm just a little jumpy today…."

The rest of the sentence escaped her. Her eyes grew large. The man stood in the center of the main aisle holding the most skittish horse in the barn by nothing but a handful of mane.

He stroked the horse's lean neck and smiled wide. "Poor guy was just walkin' up and down the aisle. Seemed lost."

Emilie's mouth fell half-open. Not only did Derrick hold Redman with so little effort, but the man had also shed his rain gear. His large T-shirt and loose-fit jeans stretched across walls of hard muscle. She sucked in a quick breath and forced her eyes up. His wide-set steely eyes, golden skin and thick waves of dark hair sticking out recklessly in every direction weren't any less appealing.

Emilie blinked and shifted her gaze to the gelding beside him. "That's Redman. He's a rescue and he's usually a bit…flighty." The one time she'd ventured to touch him, the scared animal had tried to bite her.

"Well, who can blame him? Look at this place. It's like a country club in here." He pointed to the dark stained cedar that crowned the open foyer with its cathedral ceiling and faux antler chandelier. Then he gave the chestnut a hearty pat on the shoulder. "Yep, Redman, I know how you feel."

Emilie put the blanket down and pulled at the neck of her damp sweater. "That horse belongs in Stall K and apparently he needs a snap clip on his door. Put him away, Mr. Randall. We need to—"

"I'd really like it if you could call me something besides Mr. Randall," he interrupted. "Makes me think my dad is here."

She lifted an eyebrow.

"So, just call me Derrick. Okay?" His smile grew wider.

"Okay. Derrick," she said with some reluctance.

A dimple formed on his left cheek. He turned Redman toward the north stalls and strutted away. "Be right back," he called over his shoulder.

Great.

He and the horse moved off as silently as they'd come. Emilie reminded herself to breath again. Could she really work with this guy? Did he ever stop smiling? Ugh. It wouldn't be anything like working with Camillo. But she did need help. The fact that Redman was roaming the aisles was proof of that. And Mr. Winslow liked him.

When Derrick returned, Emilie looked quickly away toward the back of the stable. "It's time to turn the horses out," she said. "But I'll show you the old barn first. If you take the job, it's where your office and tack space will be. There's a restroom, telephone and refrigerator there for your private use."

She led the way to the far end of the facility. Derrick followed close behind. She wondered if he could sense her nervousness and the strange unease that hung in the air of the stable. She scratched her neck then clasped her hands behind her back to keep them still. Or was it he that made her nervous? She glanced over her shoulder. What if he didn't even want the job? She stopped and faced him.

"Mr. Ran—Derrick...I don't really know you, but Mr. Winslow and, of course, my sister seem to think you'd be good here and I trust their judgment. I'm sure you're aware it's not usually this quiet at Cedar Oaks. There are forty-three boarders, over fifty horses, farrier visits, riding students, vet calls and lots of shows. You'd be in charge of it all... until Camillo comes back. In that case, you'd work under him through the jumper season, but he would resume teaching lessons and scheduling. Regardless, the hours are long and you'd have to work every weekend."

Derrick's grin faded slightly. "I need this job."

"And you agree to the pay we discussed?"

He nodded.

"Good then." She shook his hand. It felt strong and warm against hers. "Are you ready to move in?"

"No. I can stay for the rest of the day but I have an

appointment with the dean to sign my leave papers in the morning. I can be back tomorrow by late afternoon."

Emilie clenched her teeth. *First he's late and now he needs a day off?* Why was she agreeing to this? *Mr. Winslow*, she reminded herself. *Mr. Winslow and the Olympics.*

"That's fine." She tried to keep the irritation from her voice. "Anyway, I forgot to ask the housekeeper to run through the apartment where you'll be staying. My father wants you near the main house. I hope that's okay? Camillo lived here in the old barn, but he left everything behind and it's a mess."

Derrick grinned again and an unfamiliar warmth spread through Emilie as she finally managed to look into his gray eyes.

"I'd be happy to sleep with Redman if you asked me to," he said. "I've never been in a heated barn before. Don't tell me it's air-conditioned, too?"

Of course it's air-conditioned. Silly man. "You want to sleep with Redman? I can arrange that." She smirked.

His smile stretched so wide the dimple reappeared on his left cheek. "Ah. You *do* have a sense of humor."

Heat rose to her cheeks. She turned and strode quickly to the old barn, pushing her way through the heavy doors that divided the two structures.

"I guess the stable hand must have closed these."

Although she couldn't imagine why. "We usually leave them open."

Emilie stopped after taking two steps into the old barn.

"Is something wrong?" Derrick asked.

"I don't know… Just—those doors should be open, and this door," she pointed to Camillo's tack room door, "it should be closed and locked. In fact, it was locked yesterday. I don't know why…"

Had Camillo come back?

She rushed into the dark room, fumbling for the switch. A putrid odor stung her nostrils and robbed her of oxygen. As light flooded the space, she gasped and stumbled back.

No. Not Camillo.

But there was his body. Stiff and strangely twisted. Clearly dead. Broken boards from old jump standards lay around him. And blood.

Emilie screamed but heard nothing as she went limp down to the floor.

TWO

Derrick scooped Emilie into his arms. She'd become completely unresponsive as he carried her back to the front stable. Shock had set in. He, meanwhile, fought waves of nausea, which he feared would only worsen after witnessing such a sight.

A dead body in a stable…

It raised all sorts of questions, like why? And how? What had happened to the poor man? Who was he?

Derrick had been too worried about Emilie to really study the situation but the man was most definitely dead. The smell was enough to be certain of that. As soon as he got Emilie settled, he'd have to call the police.

He swallowed hard, forcing the agitated gastric juices back down his throat, fighting his own shock. He hadn't expected to deal with anything like this at the new stable. Not by any stretch of the imagination.

What am I doing here, Lord?

Derrick didn't know what to pray exactly, but

seeing death had thrown him from his usual state of comfort. And *that* only his Savior could restore.

Inside the front office, Derrick laid Emilie on a small couch adjacent to her desk. She made no acknowledgment of him, even when he brushed back some strands of fine blond hair caught on her cheek. Her eyes, which had earlier struck him with their vibrancy, now appeared dull and drained. But she breathed normally and seemed steady enough, so he turned away and dialed nine-one-one from her desk phone.

As they waited, he pulled a chair beside the couch and took her tiny hand in his. A single tear slid down her pale, colorless cheek. Her eyes focused on something beyond him. He followed the direction of their gaze to a photo on the wall behind him. Encased in a silver frame, the picture showed Emilie atop a large gray horse. An attractive Latino stood beside them, holding the reins and an enormous trophy. Derrick removed the picture from the wall and handed it to Emilie. She folded her arms around it, hugging it to her chest.

The former groom? *That* was whose body they'd found? The weight of a thousand stones pressed down on him. His lungs fixed tight, no air in and no air out. What had happened here?

"He must have come back for something," she whispered. "And those jump standards fell on him…."

"I should have gone in first." Derrick moistened

his dry lips and forced some air into his chest. "I'm sorry. You shouldn't have seen that."

She turned to him slowly, her eyes unfocused. "You know, we worked together for four years. All he left was a one-line note. *Had to go. Don't look for me.* That's all it said. That's it. Like he never wanted to see me again." She began to sob.

Derrick slumped with desperation. "I'm sorry, Emilie. Maybe he was sick or had a problem and didn't want you to worry."

"But I could have helped," she said with force. Anger now replacing the sorrow. "Whatever he needed…I could have helped. Why didn't he want my help?"

Derrick remained silent by her side until the police arrived. Then he showed them to the body and answered what questions he could. But it wasn't long before they had no need of him. A female police officer stayed in the office with Emilie, who lay silent on the couch. Derrick felt useless and retreated to the north wing of the stable to get out of the way. How could he help? He didn't even know the turnout routine.

After a moment, he donned a pair of gloves, found a manure fork and a wheelbarrow and put himself to work.

"I'm Detective Steele." A voice boomed through Emilie's office door, jarring her from a coma-like trance. "You must be Miss Gill. I need to speak with you, please."

Emilie sat up, looked over at the man in the doorway and waved him inside. Short and thick, he walked with a limp and one fist propped on his hip.

He came in and took a seat in the chair that Derrick had used earlier. Then he dismissed the female officer that had been in the room. "The medical examiner has arrived. He'll remove the body soon."

Emilie shivered and checked the clock on the wall. Late afternoon. She'd lain there for hours. "I gave one of the officers Camillo's family's address and phone number in Mexico. Have you called them? I would, but I don't speak Spanish very well."

"I'll call when I get back to the station. I'm sorry, Miss Gill. Mr. Randall explained that you were close to Mr. Garcia. That he worked for you for several years."

She swallowed hard, staring down at the red Turkish rug that covered her hardwood office floor. "They depend on him for support. His family. Tell them I'll forward his pay. I don't want them to worry."

"I'll be glad to do that." Steele eyed her as he took out a pad and some paper. "Can we go over a few things?"

She nodded.

"I understand Mr. Garcia recently left your employ. Is that correct?"

Emilie stood and with robotic motions, took the note Camillo had left her from her desk. She handed it to the detective. "I guess he left Friday night. I'd seen him at dinner. He said nothing about leaving. But in the morning, when he didn't show up to groom and exercise the horses, I went to the back barn, into his office and found this note. Next to it were all his keys."

"If it's okay with you, I'd like to keep the note." He took it from her trembling hands. He folded it away in his jacket pocket. "Did you and Mr. Garcia always eat meals together?"

She shrugged. "A few times a week. He wasn't just an employee. We were friends, too."

"As I said, I'm terribly sorry." He made some notes in his little book. "So, the room where you found Mr. Garcia was normally locked?"

She nodded. "It should have been. I'm certain it was closed yesterday. I assumed it was locked."

"Do you always lock all of the rooms in the stable?"

"All the tack rooms, yes. And the feed room," she said. "I'm sure you know there is a high rate of saddle theft in the area and I've heard of people stealing the pharmaceuticals, as well, which are in the feed room."

"Who else has a key to the room where you found Mr. Garcia?"

"No one. Just Camillo and me."

"Was the stable busy this weekend?"

"No. No one's here this weekend. The staff is off for Thanksgiving and almost all the boarders went out of town."

He wrote more notes in his book. "You saw Mr. Garcia Friday night. He said nothing about leaving. Then Saturday morning he didn't show up for work so you walk back to his office and find this note and his keys. Do you have these keys?"

Emilie stood again and retrieved the keys from the top desk drawer.

"That's a lot of keys," he said. "Was his office locked when you found these and the note?"

Emilie frowned. "No. But he didn't always lock his office. There wasn't anything valuable in it. He did keep the door closed."

"Was the door closed when you found the note?"

Emilie closed her eyes. The events of the weekend blurred together. "I don't...I don't remember."

"But you're sure the tack room was closed and locked? How is that?"

His accusatory tone irked her. "I said I don't know if it was locked. I assumed it was. It was closed. I remember that."

"But you can't remember if the office door was closed?"

"No," she said.

Steele stared at her while unwrapping a stick of gum and popping it into his mouth. "What are all these keys to?"

"Camillo's apartment, his office, his tack room, my tack room, the feed room and the trailers and trucks."

"How many trucks and trailers?"

"Two of each."

He counted the keys and seemed satisfied. "And since then, you've stored these keys in this office, which only you have a key to?"

"Yes. Well, actually copies of most of these keys are in the main house, too. Why?"

He ignored her question, returned the keys to her and put away his notebook. "The ME is placing time of death at sometime between 8 p.m. and midnight. I think we can assume Mr. Garcia was hit in the head with some of that equipment that hung in the rafters, but we can't determine whether or not it was accidental until we get the body in a lab. I'm going to ask that you close off that part of the stable until I get back to you." He stood and handed her a card with his contact information.

Emilie's head spun as she reached for the card. "So, what are you saying? You're not sure if it was an accident? What do you think happened?"

"Miss Gill, does it seem strange to you that your employee left without much notice?"

"Yes."

"Does it seem strange that he would come back here in the night knowing that he gave the keys to you and that you might have locked him out of those rooms?"

"I suppose it does."

"I've been doing this sort of work for fifteen years, and I think so, too."

Steele left the room.

Emilie grabbed her stomach, ran to the bathroom and was sick.

The mucking passed slowly with the horses inside. Derrick had to halter and place each one in the cross ties before he could clean and add fresh bedding. Hours passed. But the process allowed him to learn every horse's name, memorize its distinctive markings and make an educated guess at its breeding. It helped to keep his mind off the dead body and the real question that nagged his brain. *Should I take the job or not?*

The truth was he hadn't thought over the decision much before coming. There hadn't been time. Emilie had called him yesterday and here he was. When they'd spoken on the phone, she had expected Camillo to return, so he'd accepted the job as a temporary position. But now what? She would need someone permanent and he could never commit to that.

"Mr. Randall?"

Derrick stepped out of Redman's stall, Stall K, toward the low voice. A distinguished man in his mid-fifties approached. He was slender and handsome with an intelligent forehead and the same clear green eyes as Emilie.

Derrick pulled off his right glove and extended his hand. "I'm Derrick Randall."

"Preston Gill." The man scanned up then down Derrick's person. "Did my daughter ask you to do that?" He pointed to the wooden handle of the manure fork Derrick held against his chest.

"No. She didn't."

"You know that's not part of your job. She has people here who do that."

Derrick's gaze swept the interior of the stable. "Well, today, it just seems to be me."

"That's because my daughter gave everyone the weekend off." Mr. Gill spread two fingers across his short, silvery mustache and twitched his nose at the strong odor of manure beside him. "I spoke with Emilie about your employment. She says you're only here temporarily?"

Derrick stopped, placed the manure fork against the wall and removed his other glove. "Yes. For the season. Then back to school."

"I see." Mr. Gill paused and took in a long, steady breath. "Well, perhaps in light of recent circumstances, you'd consider something a bit longer term now? Think it over. I can make it worth your while. As long as you and I can come to an understanding."

Derrick frowned. "An understanding?"

"Yes. While you're in this job, there are certain things I expect you to do."

Derrick eyed the man carefully. "Such as?"

"For starters, help my daughter get on to the Olympic team."

Derrick laughed. "I don't see how I can—"

"Don't be modest, Mr. Randall," her father interrupted. "I ran a check on you. I know what you bring to the table. I've even been advised of your relationship with Peter Winslow. You could be key in securing him as her trainer."

Derrick stiffened. "You ran a check on me?"

"I'm careful about who works on the estate. And with my daughter."

"I can appreciate your concern for your daughter." Derrick moved toward Redman, still hooked in the cross ties. Taking the animal by the chin strap, he led him into his stall. "But I think you overestimate my influence over Peter. He's not likely to take a client he doesn't want just because I ask him to."

Mr. Gill took a step closer.

"There's more to what you're asking, isn't there?" Derrick narrowed his eyes.

Mr. Gill feigned a smile and stuffed his hands into his pants pockets. "You have to understand that the Gill name sometimes raises conflicts. I travel a lot and I don't want anyone taking advantage of Emilie in my absence. I need your assurance that you will watch out for her best interest, make sure nothing untoward happens."

Untoward? Derrick shook his head. "You mean you want me to babysit her."

"No." Mr. Gill looked annoyed. "My daughter

doesn't need a babysitter. But I do worry about her business, her travel, the media. Just be there. Keep things under control. Notify me if you feel a situation warrants my involvement. Mr. Garcia and I had a nice relationship. I was hoping you and I could have the same."

"So, I'd be a bodyguard? An informant?"

"Mr. Randall, I don't know if it's necessary to label this. You need money to finish veterinary school. I know your scholarship fund ran dry. So, I know you could use this." He reached into the breast pocket of his suit coat and handed Derrick five one hundred dollar bills. "And I get the comfort of knowing that my daughter is safe."

Derrick backed away, lifting both palms in the air. He did need money, but this didn't seem like an honest way to go about getting it. "Mr. Gill, no disrespect, but this doesn't seem ethical to me. I think my coming here was a mistake."

He tried to pass, but Preston Gill placed a firm hand on his chest to stop him. He leaned in close to Derrick's face and stared with large green eyes, similar to his daughter's in shape and color. But different. In Emilie's, he'd seen sadness, irritation, sometimes a flicker of playfulness. Her father's displayed nothing, keeping everything locked away.

"Think this over, Mr. Randall. I'm on the board of your university. I can make it difficult for you to return."

"Well, vet school is looking less and less appealing." The urge to laugh passed over him.

"I had a feeling you would say that. It seems you've spent your life not finishing what you start."

Derrick dropped his head. The insult stung deeply. He thought about shoving Mr. Gill off his chest. His fingers curled into fists. *Please, Lord.* He forced a deep breath into his lungs and prayed for calm.

Mr. Gill took a step back and placed the money back into his own coat pocket. "There's nothing underhanded about this, Randall. The simple truth is that as CEO of a leading financial group I travel constantly and I can't be there for Emilie. But my daughter is still important to me. I don't trust her care to anyone. Especially after such upsetting events. I want to know she's taken care of."

"Does your daughter know about this…arrangement?"

"I see no reason for that."

Derrick nodded, certain his conscience wouldn't allow him to agree to those terms. "Then my answer is no. My regrets to your daughter."

He pushed by Mr. Gill and walked straight to his car. Shaking with emotion, he stood on the concrete sidewalk in front of his ten-year-old Honda. It looked like scrap metal wedged between a shiny Escalade and a fully loaded Ford F-350.

He searched his pockets for his keys then groaned, remembering he'd left them and his rain gear next to Redman's stall. He hated to go back inside. He didn't know if he'd be able to hold back if he saw Mr. Gill again.

But Emilie. He needed to go back for her. He'd shaken hands with her. Promised to work there. She'd just lost someone she'd been close to. He shouldn't walk out without saying a word.

Derrick made his way to the Redman's stall. His rain jacket and pants lay there, his car key inside the jacket pocket. Redman poked his head over the door and stared at him with liquid eyes. He stroked the horse's face. A feeling of peace seemed to flow straight from the animal to the pit of his soul. Derrick pulled away and nearly collided into the full wheelbarrow and manure fork he'd left in the aisle.

Seems you never finish what you start. Mr. Gill's words tore at him.

Derrick rolled the waste to the compost pile then swept the concrete aisles. Afterward, he put away the equipment and walked toward Emilie's office. The drone of Preston Gill's voice filled the hallway. Derrick slowed his steps, wincing at the man's harsh words.

"You don't need to hold a memorial service."

"But, Daddy, he worked for us for four years. We have to do something. Help me. I don't know how to deal with this."

Derrick's heart twisted at Emilie's compassionate plea. Surely, her own father would be moved.

"It was a tragic accident. But there's nothing any

of us can do. And I have to go. This unplanned event has made me late for an important meeting."

Unplanned event? The man called death an unplanned event? Mr. Gill's callous attitude made Derrick itch and burn to step into the conversation. But who was he to do such a thing? He hardly knew Emilie. It wasn't his place. And now that he thought about it, she might not appreciate his interference. Best to walk away. Go home. Cool off. Think things over and give Emilie a call in the morning.

So, Derrick left. He could talk to Emilie tomorrow. She'd been through enough for one day.

THREE

Sleep would not come. Each time Emilie closed her eyes, her head clouded with distorted visions of Camillo. His twisted body. Blood.

After restless hours, she slipped from her warm bed, tossed a sweatshirt over her pajamas and wound her way through the large house. In the kitchen, on the antique secretary, she found something to busy her unsettled mind—a stack of work-related documents, waiting for her undivided attention.

Emilie forced her energy into checking receipts, preparing deposits and writing invoices. When finished, she shuffled the papers on her desk into neat piles, which uncovered a forgotten gift.

A Bible from Camillo.

The small leather-bound book had been there for months, untouched. She reached for it with a careful hand as if it might bite. Such an odd present for her twenty-fifth birthday. She did not share Camillo's newfound faith. But today, the gift brought a surge of sentiment and fresh tears to her eyes.

For the first time, she thumbed over the thin pages, finding a passage he must have underlined.

> The LORD is my rock, my fortress and my deliverer; my God is my rock, in whom I take refuge. He is my shield and the horn of my salvation, my stronghold.

Emilie traced the words with her finger, considering their meaning. How is God a deliverer? It seemed to her He allowed the people who loved Him to die. Camillo. Her mother. Where was His refuge for them?

Emilie closed the Bible and flung it on the shelf above. It missed and fell back to the desk with a thud. A sheet of paper slipped from between its pages and twirled to the floor like a white butterfly. She retrieved the paper from the terra-cotta tiles and carefully unfolded the single page.

> As much as I care for you, I can no longer continue this—us. I will keep my promise, though. I will tell no one. And trust you will do the same for me. But you must understand now that I know I can no longer help.
>
> May you find peace in the Lord who loves you.
>
> Camillo

Emilie reread the words, her hands shaking and her heart pounding against her ribs. Seeing Camillo's soft angular handwriting brought new tears to her eyes. Who was the letter to? Not to *her.* That was certain. She'd never shared a promise with Camillo. Strange, she thought, to find this now.

What else didn't I know about you, Camillo?

Placing the note on her desk, she turned away and looked out the large bay window. Morning had come and with it, she hoped, a chance to get to work and escape her heavy emotions. Quietly, she showered, dressed and headed out to the stable.

I shouldn't take the job. Derrick cradled the phone in his palm, staring down at the number to the Cedar Oaks Stables where he'd scribbled it onto the outside cover of his phone book. After all that had happened yesterday, it seemed clear he should not take the job. He needed to call Emilie right now and tell her his decision.

So, why couldn't he bring himself to dial the number?

Two days ago, he'd never heard of the stable. He knew Emilie by name only and most of what he'd heard had not been completely favorable. Now he wondered why. From what he gathered, Emilie was beautiful, intelligent and obviously capable of great friendship and love, as she had displayed in her complete devastation at the loss of her friend. Derrick had found her intriguing. In fact, he was having difficulty getting her amazing eyes out of his mind for more than seconds at a time.

He clenched his teeth. Great. He'd just given himself another reason to give up the position. And that was what he needed to do. Determined this time, he dialed the number on the phone book.

"Cedar. Cedar Oaks..."

Derrick paused at the quivering tones in Emilie's voice. "Emilie? Is that you? This is Derrick."

She didn't respond.

"Are you all right?" Derrick swallowed hard. A feeling of panic waved through him. Something felt wrong.

"Uh...yes, Derrick. Sorry, I'm fine." Her voice was icy.

She didn't sound fine. Derrick scratched his head. Poor woman, she'd probably had a terrible night. And here he was getting ready to let her down. Derrick's gut twisted as if a stone had settled in his stomach. "I'm sorry about leaving without talking to you yesterday. You were with your father when I was heading out and...well, anyway...I just wanted you to know I've been thinking this over and I'm not sure—"

"Okay. You're coming today, right?" she interrupted. "My father said you'd be back early."

What? Her father? Why would her father say that? "Emilie, what are you talking about? Are you sure you're okay?"

"Yes, and whenever you can get here is fine."

Derrick could hear the emotions in her strained voice. It wasn't just exhaustion confusing her. There was something else. Something unnatural and it was starting to concern him. "Emilie, you're not making any sense. What I was saying is that—"

"You know, Derrick," she interrupted again, "we'll have to talk when you get here. The police have arrived. I need to talk with them."

"The police?" Why would the police be back? And so early in the morning.

"Well, a forensics team is here. Okay. See you soon. You're a lifesaver."

"But what's a…" Derrick stopped. Emilie had already hung up. And it didn't matter anyway. He knew what a forensics team meant—it meant that a crime had been committed.

A strange mixture of urgency and relief spread through Derrick. *Well, God,* he thought to himself, *that's one way to tell me I'm making the wrong decision.* As quickly as he could, Derrick packed up and headed back to Cedar Oaks.

"Murdered?" Emilie could barely repeat the heinous word. How could she think after Steele had uttered such a horrific statement?

Camillo Garcia murdered?

Steele waited for Emilie to take a seat behind her desk. Then he pulled the pen and tiny notebook from his jacket pocket, just as he had the day before. "As I was saying, the coroner suspected, as did I, that your employee's death involved foul play. There will be a complete autopsy performed today, which should give us more insight. As you can imagine, I have more questions."

"Of course." She sucked in a breath, trying to hold back her emotions. With a trembling hand, she wiped her moist eyes. "I'm sorry. This is all so unbelievable...."

Detective Steele pulled his chair closer to her desk. "I understand this is difficult, Miss Gill. And it really could be as simple as Mr. Garcia having been in the wrong place at the wrong time. You said yourself that there are a lot of stable break-ins in the area."

She shook her head. "But nothing was taken."

"True. But I can't rule it out. A thief could have gotten caught, panicked, killed Mr. Garcia and run.... Now, Miss Gill, how late were you at the stable Saturday evening?"

She cleared her throat. "Until nine. But I didn't go into the old barn. I'd been there early that morning when I found the note. I didn't go back."

Steele jotted notes in his little book. He paused and looked up. "And was anyone else around, say between six and when you left?"

She shook her head. "No. Not that late on a Saturday night."

"Are you usually here that late?"

"No. Not usually. I normally leave at six. But I had a special trainer coming Sunday morning and without Camillo I had to prepare everything myself. Plus I'd given the stable hands the weekend off, since it's a holiday, so I brought the horses in and fed them myself. Anyway, the whole time I kept thinking… well, hoping that Camillo would come back…." Her voice broke off with the strain of emotion.

"And you saw nothing unusual while you were here? No cars or trucks? No workers?"

"No. Like I said, everyone was away. As far as I know, no one was here but me."

He scribbled more notes in his pad. "The estate entrance has an iron gate with a keypad entry system. Is it closed at night?"

"Yes. It closes at eight and is only accessible with a code or by calling the main house. That's what time the stable is officially closed and what time the house staff leaves. It opens again at six in the morning. But some employees know the code."

"Which ones?"

"Camillo knew it. Rosa Billings, the housekeeper. Mr. Huss, the grounds manager. And my dad's lawyer, Mr. Adams."

"Was it common for Mr. Garcia to go out in the evenings?"

"Not that I know of," Emilie said.

He nodded. "Did Mr. Garcia have many friends outside the stable?"

She shrugged. "He had a few, but his job didn't really allow for an active social life. He worked long, hard hours and he was very dedicated. I was lucky to have him. He was great at his job. In fact, I know for certain that a couple of other barns tried to woo him away."

The detective leaned forward. "Do you know which barns approached him?"

"I suspect some of my competitors. Perhaps, Jack Frahm or Leslie Raney."

"Did Mr. Garcia consider these other positions?"

"I don't know why he would have. He wouldn't have been paid any better, that's for sure."

His brow creased upward, showing his small gray eyes. "Did you pay Mr. Garcia extra money in addition to his salary to ensure his position here?"

She blinked rapidly. "No. I didn't need to. His salary was more than sufficient. That's what I was trying to say."

"So, you're denying that you gave Mr. Garcia large sums of cash on a monthly basis?"

She half laughed at the question. "Of course, I'm denying it. It's not true."

"Then you can't explain why Mr. Garcia made cash deposits every month totaling as much as five thousand dollars in addition to his check from Cedar Oaks Stable?"

"What? Camillo made cash deposits?" She shook her head from side to side. "That can't be true. He worked for me all the time. There's no way he had time to moonlight for cash."

"Uh-huh." The detective scratched his head and rubbed his broad nose. He glanced down to read something in his notebook then looked back at her. "Is there any chance Mr. Garcia was into something illegal, like drugs or gambling? The ME found a trace of drugs in his system. And it appears that his wrists had been bound for hours before death."

She felt her eyes widen. "No way. The only drugs Camillo touched were the joint supplements we feed to some of the older horses each morning. He didn't even drink. And I can't imagine he would have gambled. He sent most of his money to his family in Mexico."

"That's what he told you?"

"Yes. That's what he told me because it's the truth." Emilie frowned.

"What about enemies?" he asked. "Did Mr. Garcia have any problems getting along with the boarders or other workers here?"

"Never. Everyone loved him. Especially his riding students…" She looked up quickly. "You know, he did make some extra money riding horses for boarders and teaching lessons. Maybe that's where the extra cash came from?"

"That money is recorded since he took personal checks for that work. In fact, Garcia kept meticulous records, which is why the unaccounted five thousand in cash each month really sticks out."

Emilie twisted her lips. "Well, I have no idea."

"Yesterday, you stated that you and Mr. Garcia were very good friends." He checked his notes again. "How about elaborating?"

"Elaborating?" Emilie raised an eyebrow.

He gave a curt nod.

She shrugged. "Uh…we worked together all day, every day and we were friends. Sometimes we had meals together and we would chat." She stood, walked to the coffeepot and poured herself a full mug. "Would you like some coffee, Detective Steele?"

"No, thank you."

Emilie found her seat again and took a sip of the hot brew. The detective fell silent, staring at the collection of awards and photos on her walls.

"Look, Detective Steele, I don't have much time outside my life here at the barn and all the shows I do. Neither did Camillo. It's not surprising that over the four years he worked here we became friends." She tightened her hands around the warm mug and lifted it again to her lips.

His face pinched and his eyes rolled up at the ceiling. "Yes, I get that, Miss Gill. What I'm asking is were you intimate?"

Emilie choked on her intake of coffee and struggled not to spill the mug as she placed it on the desktop. "No. Goodness no. Camillo was handsome and very sweet, but I never felt like that about him. Really, if you'd seen us together, you'd realize how ridiculous the idea is."

"When I questioned your stable boy Gabe, he didn't seem to think it ridiculous at all. In fact, he said and I quote, 'They were a thing. They were together all the time.'" Detective Steele returned his pad and pencil to his jacket pocket and placed his hands on his knees.

Emilie gave him an angry stare. "Gabe cleans stalls and fills water buckets. That doesn't exactly make him an authority on relationships."

"No, it doesn't." He looked at her and frowned. "But I could see how being who you are, if you had a liaison with your own groom, you'd want to keep it a secret. But don't think it will stay that way. If it's the truth, it will come out in this investigation. For certain, Mr. Garcia was involved with a woman. I've looked through his apartment and there is ample evidence of that. If not you then someone else. I'll need to talk with this person. If you were such a good friend, perhaps you know her?"

Emilie thought of the letter she'd found in the Bible. Could that have been to a woman? Possibly. But wouldn't she have known if Camillo had had a girlfriend? "Mr. Steele, I promise I had no idea that Camillo was involved with someone or if he even was. In fact, I find it hard to believe. It couldn't have been serious."

He looked at her with a suspicious eye. And she realized her words had sounded like those of a jealous lover.

"Miss Gill, someone killed your friend. And my job is to find and reveal that person, no matter who it is." He stood and placed some papers on her desk. "Those are warrants to search your facility. And I'll need a list of all your boarders and staff. Camillo's friends, too."

"Sure," she said. "Whatever I can do."

"Thank you. I didn't expect you to be so compliant." He walked to the doorway, stopped and looked back at her with a smirk. "Your father has taught you well."

"What? To cooperate with the police?" She frowned. "Why wouldn't I?"

"Believe me, Miss Gill, not everyone at the top of my suspect list is quite so agreeable."

Emilie's eyes went from the warrants to Detective Steele's face. "You're kidding. How could I be a suspect?"

"You had means and motive, and you were here alone. How could you not be?" He turned and left her office.

FOUR

Derrick swept into Emilie's office at full speed and came to a screeching halt before her desk. "Are you okay? What happened?"

Emilie lifted her head and pulled the hair back from her face. She wondered how red and puffy her eyes must have been. "Of course I'm okay. How'd you get here so fast? I thought you had an appointment." The natural timbre of her voice surprised her. She'd been anything but calm when speaking to her father and his lawyer about the disturbing conversation with Mr. Steele.

"I took care of my appointment with some phone calls. You didn't sound so great on the phone. I thought I should come straight here."

He'd been worried? Emilie wiggled uncomfortably in her seat and looked away. "Oh…I'm sorry. It was a bit confusing when you called, but I'm fine…uh… help yourself to some coffee."

Derrick frowned as he made his way around the desk to the coffeemaker and helped himself.

"It might be strong," she warned him. Two hours

had passed since her conversation with Steele. Her father was on his way back home to look into things. Mr. Adams had promised to put in a call to the D.A. Still, Steele's accusatory statement continued to rattle her already fragile nerves.

He sat across the desk from her and sipped the strong coffee in silence. Emilie studied the sharp, angular line of his clean-shaven jaw. Her stomach quivered as he caught her eyes. His brows came together slowly.

"So, I was right," he said. "Something is wrong. I can see it in your eyes."

"No." She shook her head but realized it was futile to try and conceal the truth. "Okay. Yes." She sighed. "The police came back this morning to investigate further. And there's going to be an autopsy."

"An autopsy?" Derrick sat up straight and focused on her, tilting his head slightly. "Why? I thought the beams fell from the rafters and killed him."

"I guess they're not sure." She tried to look him in the eye, but she couldn't bear the intensity of his gaze. She shifted her focus to the floor. "Let me take you to your apartment. I'm sure you have things to unpack."

Derrick pressed his lips together and placed the coffee cup on the edge of her desk. "That's it? That's all they told you?"

Emilie felt nauseous. She didn't want to talk about her conversation with Detective Steele. She didn't want to think about the fact that someone might have killed Camillo. That she was a suspect. "No. That's not all…. Camillo had been tied up and they are saying he had taken drugs…" She tried to swallow. "But—I—I can't really—"

"He was tied up? So they think he was murdered?" His question sounded out in an incredulous tone.

She nodded. A rush of tears spilled from her eyes.

"Oh. Hey. Hey. I'm sorry, Emilie." He stood and dusted his palms up and down the legs of his pants. "Really. I'm sorry. Of course, you don't want to talk about it. You must be exhausted. I…uh…I should get to work."

Emilie nodded again, trying to get her voice to function. "Gabe is here doing stalls and turnout. He can show you my tack. I wrote a workout program for you…." She searched her desk for the list she'd made. But through the wall of tears, she couldn't find it. The more she searched, the more she confused the pages on her desk into a large mess.

Derrick placed his strong hands over hers, stopping them as they fumbled back and forth. "You need to go home. Get some rest. I can manage. Trust me."

"No. I—I can't. I have to—"

"Emilie, your friend just died. Go home," he repeated, releasing her hands. "I'll call you if I have a question."

"I can't. I have to call Mr. Winslow and reschedule. Actually, I need to reschedule the whole week. And we're low on sweet feed. And I need to exercise—"

"I can do those things. All of them." He walked behind her desk and rolled her chair back. "You're so tired you can barely speak. Go home. Rest. I'll drive you there."

She looked into his steely eyes. "I don't want to go home."

"Rest here then." He swung her chair toward the couch.

She stumbled the three feet to the sofa. "Okay. I'll lie down. But I won't be able to sleep."

He grabbed a throw, tossed it at her and then walked to the door.

She pulled the blanket to her chest. "You'll call Mr. Winslow?"

He looked back and nodded.

"And exercise my Grand Prix horses without getting yourself killed?" She wiped her cheeks.

"I used to ride bulls." He gave her a half smile. "I think I can handle your ponies."

"They're not ponies. They're—they're finely tuned athletes."

"I'll be good to them. Rest." The door clicked as he pulled it tight.

Emilie closed her eyes and listened to the fading click of his boots against the concrete as he strode away. Lying back, her sobs ceased but she couldn't stop Steele's questions from filling her mind.

Had Camillo been in love? Was that why he'd

left? Did that relationship have something to do with his death? Obviously, the detective thought it was important. Emilie looked at Camillo's photo on the wall.

You had a secret, she thought as sleep began to still her heavy heart. *Did it get you killed?*

Derrick found Gabe and cleared permission to ride Emilie's horses with the police. He exercised Chelsea, Duchess and Bugs—three of Emilie's four show jumpers, spectacular animals, bending and relaxing under the guidance of his leg and the touch of his soft hands. But he didn't enjoy it as he should have, not with a million thoughts racing around his head. Knowing that Camillo Garcia might have been killed was quite a shock. What if Garcia's death had been work related? Would he be next? And what about Camillo's strange "arrangement" with Mr. Gill? He hoped the police would straighten this mess out quickly and not just for his own sake, for Emilie's, too. Poor woman looked half-dead herself. Derrick pushed the many questions from his mind and forced his thoughts back to his tasks.

It had been months since he'd done so much riding in one day. At some point, his legs became as limp as cooked pasta. When he saw that Marco had thrown a shoe, he didn't think about nailing it back on. Not only did his legs need a break, he wasn't about to do anything to a horse worth a half-million dollars without permission.

Taking a seat on a large tack trunk, he pulled his cell phone from his jacket. He got Peter Winslow's number from his uncle and made the call he'd promised.

"You have a minute, Peter?"

"Certainly. I was just about to call the stable. I heard about Garcia," the trainer said. "What's the story?"

"Not a good one. Maybe murder. And the investigation is going to tie Emilie up for a few days. She wants to reschedule, if possible."

"Absolutely. She'll have to come to my place, though. I'll call back with the exact time."

"Thank you, sir." Derrick smiled. He didn't know Emilie well, but he got a good feeling when he thought about her working with Peter.

"So, you're taking the job?" Peter asked.

"Yes, sir."

"Good, then," Peter said. "See you soon."

After the call, Derrick made a trip to the supply store for sweet feed, dropped his things at his new apartment and returned to the stable. Emilie's Jeep was still stationed at the front door, but the police vehicles had departed. In their place, a new-looking Ford pickup had parked. A wave of anxiety rolled over him as he pulled in next to the truck. Gabe had gone for the day, which meant he'd left Emilie alone. What was he thinking? For all he knew, the barn was not a safe place.

Ignoring his aching legs, Derrick rushed into the

stable again and raced across the foyer to Emilie's office. He cracked the door, allowing the light to illuminate her long, blond hair, which fell over the side of the sofa. He stood there until he saw the rise and fall of the blanket as she took a slow breath. Then, he released a deep exhale of his own.

"She's asleep." A sultry voice sounded from across the foyer. Derrick jerked his head and then frowned at the tall brunette dressed in tight jeans, work boots and a flannel top stepping from Marco's corner stall. No one but Emilie or he should be poking around one of those Grand Prix horses.

"You must be Camillo's replacement." She continued toward him with deliberate steps, her figure well exposed by the shirt she'd left unbuttoned too low.

"Derrick Randall," he said, keeping his eyes fixed on her face.

"Nice to meet you." She held out a hand. "I just heard the news. So sad. I can't believe Camillo's gone. And now they're saying murder? It's unbelievable. Who would hurt Camillo? He was as gentle as a kitten. Emilie must be beside herself. And all those reporters outside the estate."

Derrick shook her hand, noting her enthusiastic expression didn't match her empathetic words. "I didn't see any reporters at the gate."

"Well, they're there now. I had to call up to the housekeeper to get in," she said.

Derrick supposed the news stations could have

arrived while he'd visited his apartment. He tried to relax. "So, you know the Gills?" he asked.

Emilie stepped out of her office, clearing her throat. "Of course she knows us. She's our vet."

The vet? Why didn't she say so? Derrick lifted an eyebrow.

"Oh, Emilie, did we wake you?" The strange woman turned to Emilie with more faux sympathy.

"No. I woke up a while ago," Emilie said.

Derrick doubted that was true.

"I'm so sorry about all this." The vet rushed over to Emilie and gave her a hug.

"Thanks." Emilie stiffened but returned the hug then stood back. "So, Derrick, this is Cindy Saunders. Dr. Cindy, this is my new groom, Derrick Randall."

Saunders. The name clicked in Derrick's head. "I've heard of you. You invented some kind of joint therapy, right? You're famous."

"Not famous." Cindy waved her palms back and forth in protest. "Emilie's the famous one around here."

Emilie ignored the insincere-sounding compliment. "Derrick is in equine veterinary school."

"Really?" Cindy's face lit with approval as she eyed him up and down. "Working and taking classes? Kind of a long commute."

He shook his head. "No, I'm on a little break

from school. So was that what you were doing with Marco? Your therapy?"

"Yes." Cindy nodded, again moving close to him.

Emilie tensed. "So, you said the media is here?"

"Yes," Cindy said with a dramatic sigh. She put her arm around Emilie and walked her toward the office. "Loads of television crews just outside the gate. It's a real circus. They stopped me and asked all sorts of terrible questions. I could barely get in."

Emilie slid from Cindy's embrace. "Great. I'd better go deal with that." She looked to Derrick. "Did you get a chance to ride?"

"I rode everyone but Marco. He threw a shoe."

"You're afraid to tack on a shoe?" Emilie smirked.

"Wasn't sure how particular you were about who took care of things like that."

"Good thinking." Emilie smiled as she stepped into her office. "Maybe Dr. Cindy would tack it on for you?"

Cindy sashayed back to Marco's stall. Her brown eyes grew wide, her gaze resting on Derrick's figure. "Emilie's letting you ride Marco on your first day?"

"Apparently so." Derrick felt the burn in his legs again.

"Camillo was fabulous on him. Do you mind if I stay around and watch? If you can get him to perform a piaffe, I'll take you to dinner."

Dinner? What was up with this lady? Flirting with him? Had she forgotten that someone had just died? "I'll get that shoe." He hurried off to the feed room.

Within a few minutes, Cindy had replaced the shoe and given the gelding an injection. She looked at her watch. "Oh. I can't stay after all. But here's James's number for you. He's the farrier. Looks like Marco could use a new set of shoes. Rain check on our dinner?"

Derrick took the card she handed him and made a noncommittal gesture. He tacked up the gelding then made his way to the schooling ring and started his warm-up with a small audience made up of after-school riders, the evening stable hands and adult boarders. They'd all gathered around to check him out and whisper about what had happened to Garcia.

They were a distraction Derrick didn't need. Marco was an explosion of power who needed precise queues from his rider. Lost in trying to control the difficult horse, Derrick almost missed the two police cars heading for the barn. And the television news van that followed.

Quickly, he dismounted, handed Marco to an evening stable hand and dashed toward Emilie's office. But already two policemen were escorting her through the front doors of the stable. One of the officers held up a hand, indicating for him to stay back.

Emilie lowered her head and looked away. "Call my lawyer. And my father."

"And tell them what?" Derrick's voice cracked through the tense air.

"Can't you guess? I'm being arrested," she said, trying to sound bravely unaffected.

Derrick could see she was close to tears. "For what?"

"For the murder of Camillo Garcia," one of the officers answered.

FIVE

"Tell me the truth, Miss Gill." Steele glared across the interrogation room at her. "Quit wasting my time."

Emilie pretended to study her neglected manicure. She refused to give the detective the satisfaction of knowing he frightened her. "I'm sorry. Did you say something?"

"I know you were in that tack room. Fingerprints don't lie. And yours were the only other prints in the room besides those of Garcia. You were the only one in the stable that night. And the only one with a key to that room."

"What about the key at the main house?" Her voice remained surprisingly calm considering how her heart pounded against her ribs.

"Locked up and accounted for. According to your housekeeper, no one's touched that key box in weeks."

"Maybe someone made a copy?"

"Maybe. But you have a key and motive," he said in a whisper.

"A motive?" Emilie closed her eyes tight, trapping the tears inside. Her hands pressed together into her lap. She forced herself to breathe. "How do you think I could—"

"Don't say another word, Miss Gill." Mr. Adams, her father's attorney, burst into the room. He looked as he always did, calm, coiffed and smug. The smell of expensive cologne and fine fabric wafted in after him. Placing his leather case on the tabletop with efficacy, he handed her a dark winter coat and a pair of large sunglasses, then he stared at the detective. "I've read over your statement, Mr. Steele. It's absurd. Judge Hayward must have been asleep when he signed that warrant. You have speculative evidence at best. My client's only care is to make the Olympic Equestrian team. Eliminating her own groom would hardly advance her progress to that end. In any case, I've posted bail and Miss Gill will be going home now. If you have any further questions for her, they go through me first."

"Then I'll be in touch." Steele clenched his jaw then exited the room.

"Please tell me this is all over now." Emilie folded over in her chair, shaking from head to toe.

Mr. Adams took the seat next to her and patted her knee. "This is a bit of a mess, actually. Mr. Steele has strong physical evidence indicating that you and Mr. Garcia were involved. He believes Garcia wanted to leave you for another woman and that you killed him in an act of rage and jealousy."

"But that's not true! How can he have evidence on something that never happened?"

"I don't know," Adams said. "But I'm afraid with the amount of time that you and Mr. Garcia spent together we might have a tough time convincing a jury."

"A jury?"

"Just thinking ahead. Now, let's get you home and rested." Adams attempted a smile.

Emilie released a shaky breath. Mr. Adams helped her from the table and into the long coat. She placed the sunglasses atop her head and followed the lawyer through the station. They passed Steele in the hallway.

"This isn't over," the detective sneered.

Mr. Adams ignored the detective and continued to escort Emilie to the back door. "Until there's another suspect, I'm afraid that man is going to make a nuisance of himself—one of those cops that thinks anyone with money has something to hide."

"Daddy is not going to be happy about this," Emilie said.

"Don't worry about your father." Mr. Adams patted her shoulder. "Or about yourself. We'll have this all taken care of."

She nodded slowly, wanting to believe him but hearing, all the same, what he left out. Her father would get the charges against her buried. But what about Camillo? Who would find his killer if the police were only investigating her?

"So, the local news station is parked out front," Adams continued. "I arranged for your family limo to sit there as a diversion. Mr. Randall is parked around back and he will drive you home."

Derrick? Her shoulders drooped low. "Why him?"

"No one knows him or his car." Mr. Adams pointed to a black compact as they stepped outside.

Derrick stood beside the small car. He gave her a wave, a pleasant expression fixed on his face. Emilie wanted to sink into the ground.

"Go straight home. Your father's orders."

Emilie stared after the lawyer as he turned back into the police station.

"Come on, girl. It's freezing out here." Derrick's accent seemed extra-thick.

She forced her shoulders back, breathed in the crisp November air and pulled the sunglasses down over her eyes as she turned to face him. Derrick held the passenger door open with an overly gallant gesture. She climbed in, wondering what he must be thinking of her, of this job and this big mess he'd landed himself into. Did he consider for one second that she was a killer? Did anyone? The mere idea made her shudder.

Derrick hopped in the driver's side and revved the engine. "Sorry about the car. Mr. Adams insisted I drive it."

"Do you really think I'm worried about the kind of car I ride home in?" She glanced sideways at him.

Didn't he realize she had far worse things to consider? That the detective would be after her again, or worse, her father would have the whole thing swept under the rug. "You seemed pretty relaxed about picking up an alleged killer."

"Yeah, right." Derrick snorted.

Emilie studied him. There was no tension, no doubt in his expression. Did he really not have any suspicions? "How can you be so sure? It's not like you really know me."

"I know enough." He grinned. "You beat people in a riding ring, not over the head with jump rails. I've always been a good judge of character, Emilie. You're no killer."

"Well, that's the nicest thing anyone has said to me all day." A warm tingling sensation rippled through her, a little hope filtering through her doubts and fears. "Wish Detective Steele could see it like that. But he has my fingerprints and fabricated motive."

"Relax, Emilie," he said. "The truth will win out in the end."

"I guess." She swallowed hard. "Did you talk to Mr. Winslow?"

Derrick guided the car through the busy parking lot. "I did. He'll call back and set something up. I also talked to some of the boarders. They got together and planned a service for Camillo."

"A memorial service for Camillo?" A lump bulged in her throat.

"Yes. Tomorrow afternoon at Community Christian."

"But…" She turned to Derrick. His gray eyes were soft and tender. "You did that? How did you know?"

Derrick pressed his lips together, keeping his eyes ahead.

"You overheard the conversation with my father."

Derrick gave a slow nod. "I did. A little of it, anyway. But I can't take credit. It was Mrs. Kecksin's idea. All I did was say that I thought you'd approve."

They turned the corner of the police station. Television crews lining the street came into view. Reporters and cameramen hovered around her father's limo. None of them noticed Derrick's car. Emilie still slumped down low in the seat.

"Ah. Now I see why he wanted me to drive my car," Derrick laughed. "Wow. Is your life always this…?"

"Messed up?" she suggested.

"I was going to say eventful."

She slid the glasses down her nose and cut her eyes at him.

A subtle grin had spread over his lips. He looked down at her. "I meant that you're keeping it together pretty well," he said. "I was expecting hysterics."

"Well, they teach us how to deal with these types of things in finishing school." A newfound calmness settled around her. She smiled for the first time that day and sat up again.

Derrick chuckled. "You know, you're not quite what I expected."

"Ha. I'm sure this whole job isn't quite what you expected."

"You've got that right." His smile widened, displaying the one dimple. "But God brought me here. So I know something good will come of it. Just wait and see."

She dropped her head in her heads. "Easy for you to say. You haven't been accused of murder."

"That's true. I haven't. But I know what I'd do if I were you."

"What's that?" she asked.

"I'd help the detectives find the truth."

"What are you talking about?"

"If your friend was killed, there has to be a reason," he said. "If Detective Steele is looking in the wrong direction, maybe you should help him look in the right one."

"But I don't know who could have killed Camillo."

"No. But you knew him better than anyone else. You'd know where to start looking."

"I don't want to play detective," she said.

"Okay. Just saying that's what I would do if I were you."

"Well, you're not me."

"I would pray, too," he added, ignoring her last statement.

"I don't really do that." She waved a hand through the air.

Derrick frowned. "It's pretty simple. You just talk to God like you're talking to me. You should try it."

"Maybe," Emilie said, ready to change the subject.

Derrick nodded and fell silent until they drove onto the Gill estate. "To the stable or home?"

"Home."

Emilie didn't know why but she did not look at Derrick or thank him when she climbed out of the car.

Derrick watched Emilie weave through the beautiful gardens behind her home. The back door opened to her—perhaps the housekeeper had come to greet her. At least she wasn't alone. She turned and closed the door to the house without looking his way. Not even a wave. Derrick wasn't sure why that bothered him but it did.

He sighed long and hard then backed up and headed to the stable. He wanted to meet with the evening stable worker and follow up on a few things he'd started earlier. But it was later than he'd realized. Stephan, the scheduled stablehand, had already left. All the horses had been brought in, fed and watered, except for Emilie's. That was his job. He started with the ladies, Duchess and Chelsea. Then he fetched Marco and finally the stallion. He couldn't help but stare at the yellow crime scene tape strung up near Bugs's stall, blocking the entrance to the old barn. What had really happened there behind that tape?

"Ho there."

Derrick started at the strange, deep voice, thinking himself the only person in the stable. He dropped the stallion's hoof that he'd been ready to pick and walked to the door of the stall.

"Got a call about one of the Gill horses."

Down the aisle, a tall man stood, legs apart and hands on hips. He was deeply tanned and dressed in a leather apron—the farrier.

"Yes. Yes, you did." Derrick stepped out of the stallion's stall, locked the door and moved toward the man. "That would have been me. I'm Derrick Randall, the new groom."

"James Joyner."

They shook hands.

"I'd thought maybe I'd missed you. I had to go out for a bit." Derrick led him to Marco and showed him the shoe Cindy had tacked on earlier.

"No. Got tied up at a new stable." Joyner inspected all four hooves. "Looks to me like he could use a new set."

"You have time for that tonight?"

"I'm here, ain't I?" James grinned then headed to his truck. "Meet me at the west doors."

Derrick pulled Marco from his stall and headed to the side entrance where James would back up his truck to work. In no time, the farrier was hunched over, pulling Marco's back leg between his knees and removing the old shoe. Then, holding a foot-long rasp in his hands, he filed over the hoof with long smooth strokes. James's hands were marked with cuts and scrapes. Sweat dripped from his forehead as he muscled through the layers of thick hoof.

Marco misbehaved. He knocked Derrick with his enormous head, then jerked his legs from James, striking a structural column to his rear.

"Is he always so restless?" Derrick asked. "He seemed to have better ground manners earlier."

"Not gonna say he's my best client." James chuckled and wiped the sweat from his face. "I heard there's been a lot going on at the stable. Maybe he's just a little shaken up."

"Maybe."

"So, how was it here today?" James asked. "I heard the cops are saying that Garcia was killed? Sounds crazy to me. I mean, who'd want to kill a groom? No offense."

"None taken." Derrick frowned, suspecting the farrier had hustled to Emilie's stable more to get the skinny on things than to work. "I was wondering the same thing myself."

"I'm sure you were." James laughed. "How does it feel taking the job of a guy who's been killed?"

"You think his death had something to do with his work?" Derrick shifted his weight.

The farrier dropped Marco's leg to the floor and stood upright. "Hey, man, I don't know. So, did they really arrest Emilie Gill?"

Derrick studied the man and considered a subtle answer. "She's home now. I didn't catch all the details."

James went back to work on the horse. "I saw Mr. Gill's Escalade and some other fancy car heading up to the main house when I came in. Probably getting ready for some big defense powwow. You're new here, but you'll see how it all works. That Mr. Gill, he may look fancy, but he's about as low as they come."

Derrick's jaw clenched. "What do you mean?"

"Preston Gill? Crooked as a corkscrew. Got everyone in his pockets. Law enforcement included. Makes me sick to think of it." James wiped his hands on the leather apron, selected a new shoe and sauntered over to his torch. As the shoe turned red under the blue flame, he hammered and bent the metal then fired it again. When he liked the shape, he doused it in a bucket of cold water. It sizzled, releasing a puff of steam into the air. He glanced back at Derrick. "You know, Garcia and I were friends, but I'm afraid that maybe he was in Gill's pockets, too. I don't know what he did for the old man but I saw Camillo take a wad of cash from him once. I didn't ask about it because it looked like they didn't want anyone seeing 'em."

"Are you saying that you think Mr. Gill asked the groom to do something illegal?"

"I don't know about that. It did look a little sneaky though." James walked back to the horse. "Why? Did he ask you to do something illegal?"

"Not that I'm aware of."

James laughed and gave Derrick a little punch to the arm. "Aw, man…I'm just foolin' with ya. But I would stay on the man's good side. You know, be good to Emilie. Even though I know firsthand she can be hard to work for. She's gotten fierce with me more than once over a trim she didn't like. But that Mr. Gill, he don't let anyone mess with his family. Like when his wife died in that car accident. A bunch of people said she'd been drinking. Well, he took care of that right away. And this place got locked up like Fort Knox. So, if they're saying his daughter killed Garcia, then my guess is within a week, those charges will be wiped off the plate and no one around here will even mention what may or may not have happened."

James gave Derrick a knowing look then bent over and nailed on the new shoe.

In her father's office, Emilie sat near the gas fireplace in a tall wingback chair. She sipped hot tea and chewed on the end of a nail. Mr. Adams and her father, seated close around his desk, drank fifty-year-old Scotch and discussed her situation as if she weren't in the room.

"Time of death is estimated between eight and eleven Saturday night," the lawyer said. "She has no alibi for that time. No one saw her. No one even spoke to her on the phone. She even told them she was at the stable alone until nine."

"But how could she overcome someone like Garcia?" her father said. "It's ridiculous."

"The ME says he was tied up and drugged before death. Traces of Ace in his system."

"What's that? What's Ace?"

The two men looked at Emilie.

"It's a drug used to calm horses when they become overly agitated," she explained.

"Do you have that at the stable?" Adams asked, wide eyed.

"No. I don't keep any. Never needed it," she said.

"Well, that's a relief." Her father, sweating uncharacteristically, pulled a hanky from his breast pocket and wiped the wetness from the sides of his face. "I still don't get the motive. Doesn't there have to be a motive before they can warrant an arrest?"

Adams glanced at her nervously. He must have bought into the idea that she and Camillo had been an item and was afraid to deliver the news.

"Daddy." She stood from her chair and walked to his desk. "They suspect that Camillo and I were a secret couple and that we had some sort of lovers' spat. It's not true, of course. Not any of it."

"So, there's no evidence of this?" He sat back in his chair and looked up at her.

She looked at Mr. Adams.

"This is another problem. They found things in Garcia's apartment, like a pink toothbrush, a women's hairbrush and lipstick," Mr. Adams said. "And he had a lot of cash, which they think Miss Gill supplied him."

Her father frowned deeply. "Items like lipstick and a toothbrush would have traces of DNA, right?"

"The lipstick and toothbrush appear to be new. Unused."

"And the brush?" her father asked.

Mr. Adams's face twitched. "The hairbrush had two strands of your daughter's hair."

Emilie fell back into a nearby chair. Fear pulsed through her veins. "That's crazy! I never even went inside Camillo's apartment."

They gave her a doubting look.

"Okay, once. Because he'd slept in and wouldn't answer his phone. It was about a year ago and I was inside for about three minutes. Long enough to find out he had the flu. I'm sure it's not my hairbrush. You know, anyone could get a piece of my hair from my riding helmet. It's always yanking out a strand or two when I remove it. And I know it's not my lipstick. I use gloss. More importantly, there was nothing but friendship between Camillo and me. I loved him like a brother. Nothing more."

"If you're telling the truth, Miss Gill," said the lawyer. "Then someone has set you up and done a jolly good job of it."

SIX

Emilie sat at the kitchen table watching for Derrick to drive her to the church for the service. Camillo's Bible sat on the table in front of her. Her hand lay on the leather cover as if touching it could bring her friend closer. Could make sense of the mess that had taken over her life.

Last night, her father and Mr. Adams had eventually pretended to believe her when she'd explained that she had no relationship with Camillo other than friendship. But their actions stated otherwise. They'd planned to make certain that "friends" in the government misplaced the hairbrush evidence and closed up the investigation. But why do that when she was completely innocent? And what would hiding evidence do to catch the real killer?

Memories of her mother's accident filled her mind. Her mother had stormed out of the house after arguing with her father. She and her father had been drinking and there was an accident. Her father had spun the story, putting the blame on another car, another driver. In the end, her mother had died in the hospital and the other driver had gone to jail for involuntary manslaughter. Now Emilie wondered if that had been the truth. Maybe her father had covered that up, too.

She rubbed her temples and fluttered her eyes, trying to bring a new, pleasant thought to her mind. No sense in dwelling on what she couldn't change. Her father would do what her father would do. It had always been that way. And anyway, the hairbrush wasn't hers. Taking it out of evidence was not exactly an injustice. Right? She hadn't killed Camillo.

But someone had. Someone had killed him right in her own stable. And nothing was going to be done about it. A steady throbbing struck against her skull.

A horn sounded in the distance. Emilie looked out across the garden. Derrick had pulled up in one of the Cedar Oaks trucks. She started for the door but glanced back at the Bible, struck with a notion to take it along. *How silly.* She turned away, grabbed her small purse and headed out.

"Thanks for driving." She climbed inside the spacious cab.

Derrick looked over with a soft expression. "I figured you had enough on your mind and I didn't know how to get to the church."

She nodded. "I was surprised you wanted to come. You didn't know Camillo."

"No. But I know you."

Derrick drove away from the house and headed

down the long gravel drive to the entrance. Emilie played with the hem of her skirt, straightening it over her knees. Green pastures blurred by the windows. A light rain began to fall as they reached the edge of the estate. Derrick fumbled around the dash. After watching him poke at almost every knob, she pointed to the wipers switch.

"Thanks. Lots of bells and whistles on this thing."

She smiled. "Camillo hated this truck. He always drove the Ford."

"Really?" Derrick looked shocked. "Wow. If I ever start my own clinic, this is exactly what I'm going to buy."

"I picked it out."

"I'm not surprised. You look like a woman who can spot quality with her eyes closed. That new Warmblood of yours is spectacular. I've never ridden a horse with that much raw talent. I watched you work her this morning. Just beautiful. She is truly a special creature. Did you go all the way to Ireland to pick her out?"

"I did. I saw a few videos of her first. Then I flew over and took a test drive." Emilie smiled, appreciating his effort to keep her mind on happy thoughts, even if it wasn't working. "I noticed all the work you did yesterday without my help or even any instruction. And my horses felt great this morning. Mr. Winslow was right. You are more experienced than I had expected."

"You weren't too sure, were you?" he teased.

"Not at all." She let out a light chuckle. A little heat rose to her cheeks. "But I should have been. My sister told me you ran your uncle's stable for years and rode on the circuit for a while. And then Mr. Winslow was singing your praises…I didn't think that man ever complimented anyone."

"Who, Peter? You've got him all wrong. He's a little stuffy on the outside but he's really just an old teddy bear. You'll see."

She sighed. "That is, if I ever get a chance to get to work with him."

"You will," he said. "So, when's the first show?"

"In a week." Emilie slumped in her seat at the thought. A week. Would all this be over in a week? "But with this investigation…I don't know. I don't think I'll be able to focus."

"A lot can happen in a week," he said.

"You know, I've been thinking about what you said. About finding the truth for myself."

Derrick gave a single nod of the head. "Any idea where to start?"

She shrugged. "Not really. We can't look through Camillo's things because the police have it all blocked off."

"That's true. But we could talk to people that knew him."

"We?"

"Sure. I can help. If you'll let me, that is."

"Can I stop you?" Her words were teasing but the

nervous tension inside her made them sound harsh. "I'm sorry. I didn't—"

"It's okay." He put his hand on hers and gave her a reassuring squeeze as he pulled up to the front of the church.

Emilie hopped out of the truck and looked back at Derrick before closing the door. Her lower lip quivered. Tears misted her eyes.

"It's going to be okay," he said.

"I wish I could believe that." She closed the door softly and walked into the church.

Derrick followed Emilie into the sanctuary, watching as tension slithered up Emilie's small frame and her hands began to tremble. Her brow creased. The desire to tuck one of her tiny hands inside his own shortened his breath and dried his throat.

He wondered what had made her change her mind about looking into things. Her father? The farrier had been right about him coming home and about a guest at the house. Derrick had seen their cars when he'd gone home to his new apartment. But Mr. Gill hardly seemed the type to encourage Emilie to investigate on her own.

In the church aisle in front of him, Emilie located Mrs. Kecksin through the small crowd and walked to her. Derrick had met the older woman earlier. She seemed to care deeply for Emilie, and appeared to be worried about the loss of her mother and now Camillo, and how that would affect her. Poor Emilie.

To have lost two people so close to her in such unexpected ways.

"Thanks for setting up the service and getting those beautiful flowers." Emilie hugged the woman close.

"You're very welcome, dear," Mrs. Kecksin said. "But I didn't provide the flowers. They're from Cindy, the vet." The woman took Emilie's hand and pressed it into her own as he had thought to do. A ping of jealousy caused Derrick's teeth to clench.

Soft hymns filled the air. Emilie and Mrs. Kecksin moved to one of the front pews. Derrick fell in behind and fixed on the soft words of the minister. He wondered how they might affect the young woman in front of him, the woman who didn't want to talk to God about her troubles. He prayed for her peace and happiness, and as he did, felt renewed with a peace of his own—his coming to work for Emilie would be a good thing. He believed it and trusted in the Lord to make it so.

As everyone filed out of the church, Emilie stayed alone in her pew, head down, staring into her lap. Derrick waited by the doors to the sanctuary.

Mrs. Kecksin stopped next to him. "I think the minister would like to speak with Emilie, if she's up to it."

Derrick turned to face the older woman. "Does she attend here?"

"Emilie?" Mrs. Kecksin's eyes opened wide. "No. I don't believe Emilie is inclined to attend any church. But Camillo did for the past few months. He became very close with the minister." She paused and looked at Emilie, still seated in the pew. "Thank you for coming with her. She'll be lost for a while without Camillo." She patted him on the shoulder and walked on.

From the side door, a short, bald man approached Emilie with quick steps. Derrick recognized Detective Steele and raced down the main aisle to stop him from approaching Emilie. She didn't need to deal with him there in the church. Really, what could he be doing at Camillo's service anyway?

"Good afternoon, Miss Gill," Steele said, reaching Emilie too quickly.

"You're not to talk to me without my lawyer present." She stood and straightened her shoulders.

"I'm not here to talk to you," he said. "I'm here to speak with him." He pointed to Derrick.

Emilie turned, looked away from Derrick and left the sanctuary.

"I just have a few questions," Steele continued.

Derrick widened his stance. "I don't suppose I need to point out how inappropriate it is that you're here?"

Steele adjusted the belt around his ample waistline. "I always attend the services of victims," he said proudly. "Profilers believe killers are often nearby. Actually, I find it interesting that *you* came to Garcia's service, seeing as you didn't know him."

Derrick stared down at him, his brows pressing together. "What do you want?"

Steele cleared his throat. "I'd like to know if your terms of employment at the stable are the same as Mr. Garcia's."

"I wouldn't know," Derrick said. "I am unfamiliar with Mr. Garcia's agreement."

"But you came to replace him? And arrived just before the body was found?"

"I came that day to help with the trainer and talk to Emilie about filling in until Garcia returned. It's a temporary position. Even now I'm here on a temporary basis."

"As an assistant to Miss Gill?"

"I'm her personal groom and exerciser. I'm also in charge of the stable when she's not available. And I'll teach lessons to some of the boarders."

"Uh-huh." Steele shifted his eyes. "And what about employment with Mr. Gill?"

"Mr. Gill?" Derrick's pulse spiked. "I don't work for Mr. Gill."

"Then why did he order a background check on you?"

"I assume because I'm working closely with his daughter."

"And how close is that? I understand you've been given an apartment at the main house."

"My apartment is over the five-car garage. About two hundred yards from the main house." Derrick spoke with a flat voice. "And I don't think they've given it to me."

Steele rolled his eyes. "Have you seen any illegal activities on the estate since you arrived?"

"No."

Steele sniffed and wiped his wide nose. "You're new in town, Mr. Randall. I know you didn't know any of these people before Sunday. But let me tell you something—the Gill family is not what they seem." He reached his stubby fingers into his breast pocket and handed Derrick a business card. "Call me if you see or hear anything." He turned and walked away, leaving a dank emptiness in the air.

Derrick waved it away and turned to find Emilie.

SEVEN

"Mr. Lucas, thank you for your services today. I know you didn't have much notice to prepare." Emilie faced the slender man that had led the memorial for Camillo. Standing at the front doors to the church, he'd been impossible to avoid. No doubt by design. She appreciated his time, but why did she have to talk to him? She didn't want his pity or his spiritual guidance, no matter how well intended it was.

The minister took her hand, still trembling with emotion, and squeezed it gently. "You must be Emilie. I had hoped to meet you today. Camillo spoke of you often."

The man did not smile but his eyes were gentle as they connected with hers. They were dark and intelligent and looked tired as though he'd seen too much and slept too little. There was no pity in them. Instead, his expression betrayed concern.

"Camillo often spoke of you, too," she said.

Derrick approached slowly as if not to interrupt. She waved him closer, hoping the minister would let them pass.

"This is my new groom, Derrick Randall," she said. "I hired him after I found Camillo's note about leaving."

"Nice to meet you." Lucas shook Derrick's hand. "If I could, I'd like to speak with you both in private."

Both of us? She glanced at Derrick, who also looked surprised by the request. A chill spiraled down her back as they followed the preacher down a wide hallway and into a cozy sitting area. Lucas motioned to the sofa and walked to the opposing chair. He let out a short frustrated breath.

"Do you know something about Camillo's death?" Emilie read tension in the lines across the pastor's brow.

"No. Not directly, anyway." Lucas stood again and paced the small room. "I know that Camillo was afraid. For himself and for you, Miss Gill."

"Afraid for me?" Emilie's blood raced through her veins. "He did seem a bit withdrawn before, but… well, I suppose it could have been fear."

The pastor sighed with disappointment. "You don't know what it was about, either?"

"No, I don't." Heat rushed to her head. "I don't know anything. I don't know why Camillo left. I don't know why he came back. I don't know how he had extra cash in his account or who his girl-friend was. If he even had a girlfriend…I'm starting to think I didn't know Camillo at all."

"Miss Gill, I know this is upsetting and I'm sorry

for that." He took his seat again. "Like I said, I had hoped you'd know something, but I didn't expect you to."

Derrick patted her hand. "This is interesting information, Emilie. If Camillo was afraid, then he *knew* he was in trouble. In danger, even. He probably didn't tell you anything because knowing would have put *you* in danger, too."

"I agree," said Lucas. "I don't mean to sound ominous but that's why I wanted to talk to you both. I fear for you, Miss Gill. You could still be in danger. And you, Mr. Randall, perhaps, by taking his position. I don't know. I'm just telling you what I feel in my gut. I wish I'd pushed Camillo to share more when we talked. I didn't."

"This is such a confusing mess." A few tears streamed down Emilie's cheek and she wiped them with the back of her hand.

"I'm sorry, Miss Gill. But know this—Camillo cared very deeply for you. He said you were the little sister he'd always wanted. And he prayed for you often. And, even though I don't know *why* he was leaving, he did tell me that he was headed to California. He told me that he had a job lined up there."

Emilie closed her eyes. She didn't want to hear any more. To learn of all these secrets he'd kept from her hurt. She stood and turned to Lucas. "Thank you for your concern."

Derrick stood beside her. "We should go. She's exhausted."

Derrick stopped and shook the man's hand. "Do you know any other friends of Camillo's that might have more information? Anything that might give Emilie some peace?"

Lucas pressed his lips together and started to shake his head. Then his face relaxed and he lifted a finger in the air. "He was part of a Bible study group. I think they hung out a bit. If you call the office tomorrow, I'll have the secretary give you their names. And, Miss Gill, Camillo didn't have a girlfriend. Not anymore. That I'm sure of."

The pastor followed them to the door. "I pray you'll be careful. And safe."

Derrick noticed the way Emilie tensed and frowned, but she said nothing, just nodded stiffly and walked away.

Derrick drove back to the estate, sensing Emilie's high emotions as she sat quietly in the seat next to him. He thought over her reaction to the minister's promise to pray for her and remembered Mrs. Kecksin's implication that Emilie had no interest in God. Was that why church seemed to make her tense? He'd thought it was her nerves and her sadness over Camillo. Yesterday, he'd not been pleased about her passive attitude on prayer. And now he wondered. Wanted to know the truth about how she felt about God.

"So…uh…you don't go to church there, huh?"

"Figure that out all by yourself?" She cut her sharp green eyes at him.

Derrick rubbed his hands loosely around the soft leather of the steering wheel, as if it could release some of the tension that seemed trapped inside the truck. "I just meant I was surprised you and Camillo didn't attend the same church."

"I don't attend any church," she said. "It's like I said before, I don't really do the God thing. And I don't want to talk about it right now."

Disappointment filled Derrick's soul. He didn't want to believe her. His mind searched for some alternative explanation. "Because it reminds you of Camillo?"

"No, because right now I can't think about anything besides the preacher telling us that we're in danger." Her jaw clenched tight. "Did you forget? He included you in it, too. And he wasn't joking."

Derrick wiped his mouth. "No. I didn't forget. But I don't figure getting all worked up about it will do much good. I take my problems to the Lord."

"You're not the least bit worried?"

Derrick let out a deep sigh. "Yes, Emilie. I'm worried. That's not what I meant. I don't think worry solves anything. I think prayer and action do. So, instead of being afraid, we should pray and we should think about who else besides Pastor Lucas might know something about Camillo so we can talk to them."

Emilie wrapped her arms around herself. "You thought what he said was helpful?"

"Yes, we learned a lot from Pastor Lucas. We learned that Camillo died trying to protect you, by leaving and not telling you what he knew. Now, we need to figure out what you're in danger of. Figure out Camillo's secret. It probably had something to do with you."

"How do you know it had to do with me? How do you even know there is a secret?"

"Because it makes sense. He was your close friend and he didn't tell you where he was going. He barely even told you *that* he was going. He knew you'd be suspicious. Ask questions. He was keeping *something* from you. The pastor said whatever it was had him afraid. Afraid for his life. And I think he died trying to keep the secret and you safe."

Emilie lowered her head. "But who would he have a secret with? Someone at the stable? He lived there, ate there, worked there."

"It's possible."

"Well, that's just too creepy to think about. That someone we know killed Camillo? Ridiculous."

"But possible."

Emilie blew out a long sigh. "I need a vacation."

"How about one to Winslow Farms in Warrenton?" Derrick grinned.

"Mr. Winslow called?" She looked up, a tiny spark of hope in her eyes.

"I talked to him this morning. He says you can come up tomorrow, if you're feeling up to it."

"Really?…Oh, but wait. I don't think I'm allowed to go anywhere."

"Warrenton is fine. I cleared it with Mr. Adams."

"Then I think Winslow's is the best idea I've heard in weeks."

"All right then. I'll have your trailer ready first thing in the morning." Derrick pulled up in front of her home.

She released her seat belt and slowly looked over at him. Her eyes were wonderfully wide and green. Salty streaks traced her pale cheeks and her lips shimmered like frosty peaches. Derrick forced his eyes to the gearshift and placed the truck in park.

"What did Steele ask you?" she whispered.

Derrick shrugged. "He just wanted to know if I had the same job as Camillo. I told him I didn't know."

"He came all the way to the service to ask you that?" Emilie lifted a brow.

Derrick shrugged. "I guess so."

"Okay. Well, if you really want to help me, I thought of something you could do."

"Anything."

"You could call the church tomorrow and find out about that Bible study for me."

"I sure could." His eyes wandered back to hers.

"Thanks," she said. "And thanks for the ride."

Derrick watched Emilie walk through the gardens to the house, chastising himself for staring.

Wow. Beautiful. He sucked in a quick breath. *And my boss. And rich. And not for me.*

Derrick headed up the stairs to his new apartment. He closed the French doors behind him. The click of the lock echoed through the large open space. Before changing back to his work clothes, he headed to the kitchen for a drink. Running a hand down the granite countertop, he noticed that someone had straightened the pile of books he'd left there and cleaned his breakfast dishes from the sink.

He opened the refrigerator and shook his head. The once empty shelves were now stocked with everything from sodas to cauliflower. Not a bad perk, free groceries and cleaning. He reached for a power drink, but his fingers grazed over a thick envelope blocking his path. He slid the packet from the shelf and peeked inside. Ten one hundred dollar bills and a note.

For your change of heart.
PG

EIGHT

"You don't have to go with me." Emilie checked the hitch then moved behind the trailer where Derrick had finished loading her horses. "I've pulled the trailer plenty of times on my own. I can make it to Mr. Winslow's without you."

Derrick cast a doubtful look at her as he secured the back doors. He stuck his hand in the air, palm up, and watched as a few snowflakes landed on his worn, leather glove. His eyes flashed from the flakes to her face. "I'm sure you can pull the trailer just fine. But I'm coming with you. It's what you pay me to do."

"Why? Because of the snow? The storm is going to blow over. I listened to the forecast. 'No accumulation.' You should stay here and work. I pay you to do that, too."

A strong gust swirled a cloud of white between them. Cold whooshed about her exposed neck. She pulled the hood of her jacket over her head.

"Look around, Emilie. The weather people are wrong. Call Peter and ask to reschedule."

"No way. Not again." She pulled the key to the truck from her coat pocket.

"Okay. But I'm going with you." He snatched the key from her hand.

"Why?" she asked, although she knew the answer. She had not forgotten the preacher's words. Obviously, he had not either. So much for his big claim not to worry.

He gave her a stern look.

"Fine. Come if you have to." Her angry grunt turned to steam in the air. "But I'm driving." She snatched the key back from his fingers, pushed past him, hopped into the truck and cranked up the engine.

Derrick rushed to the passenger door and climbed in. "Wow. You are cranky this morning. Even for you," he teased. "Is the coffeemaker broken?"

Emilie rolled her eyes at the little joke.

Derrick unzipped his coat and pulled off his gloves. He popped the knitted cap off his head and his dark hair stuck out in every direction. The nonstyle of it reinforced his I-don't-care-what-anyone-thinks attitude. Why did he seem so happy all the time? She found it distracting. Just like that stupid dimple of his. She didn't need distracting. What she needed was to forget about what had happened over the past few days and get back to riding.

"I'm not cranky. I need to focus before I ride. If you keep talking, then I can't do that."

"You know what I think?"

She looked the other way. "No, but I have a feeling you'll tell me."

"I think you're upset because Camillo isn't here to go with you. Because you're stuck with me instead."

"That's not it…at all." Her jaw clenched. After all, wasn't Derrick a six-foot-three reminder that Camillo was gone?

Hitting a patch of ice, the trailer slipped and tugged the truck to the right. She overcorrected. The front tire swerved off the path.

"You sure you don't want me to drive?" Derrick looked over at her.

"Positive."

"Well, if you change your mind let me know." He scooted low in his seat, rested his chin on his chest and closed his eyes.

Emilie eased the truck and trailer onto the main highway. Snow fell harder and in smaller and smaller flakes. Ready to turn to ice with a one-degree rise in the temperature.

Derrick had been right and the weather people wrong. Snow stuck fast to the roads and was growing deeper by the minute. Her white knuckles gripped the steering wheel tightly. "So, okay. You were right," she said after driving for thirty minutes in silence.

Derrick sat up. "About what?"

"About the Camillo thing. I miss him. He had a way of getting me to calm down before big moments. Did you call the church this morning?"

"I did. The secretary is contacting the members of Camillo's study group and making sure it's okay to give out their names and numbers. It's a privacy issue. But she thinks they will agree."

Emilie nodded.

"I met James Joyner the other night," he added. "You know, I told you I'm usually a good judge of character but I couldn't quite figure that guy out."

"I don't meet with him much. He seems uneasy around me, but always nice. Camillo liked him and he does great work."

"Yeah, I'm sure you're right. I was tired last night. Not a good way to meet someone new." Derrick sighed. "Why don't we talk about something more relaxing?"

She shrugged. "Like something besides the barn?"

He clapped his hands together. "Exactly. So what things interest the rich and talented Miss Emilie Gill?"

"Besides horses?"

"Yup. Besides horses," he repeated.

"Okay. I'll tell you." She cut her eyes at him. "But you can't laugh."

"Why would I laugh?"

"Promise not to laugh or I won't tell you."

"Okay. I promise not to laugh."

"I like to cook."

Derrick snickered.

She glared at him. "I knew you would laugh."

"I'm sorry. I'm really sorry. I didn't expect that," he chuckled.

"I know. You thought I was going to say getting a manicure or shopping at Saks."

"No." He forced the words out between laughs. "No. It's just—"

"Well, fine then. I always cook on Sunday nights after shows for everyone who helps. I'll be sure not to include you."

"Oh, come on now. That's a truly cruel thing to say to a starving bachelor. I take back my laughter."

"You can't take it back. You already laughed."

"And I said I was sorry."

"Humph." She glanced away, keeping her pouty face but grinning inwardly. The conversation was silly, but it had helped her relax. "So, what about you?"

"Me? I can't cook. I can microwave. Does that count?"

"No, I mean, what do you like? Besides horses."

"Oh. Now, there's a question without an interesting answer."

"What do you mean? You don't like anything besides horses?"

"No. I like everything. And it's a bit of a problem because I have trouble focusing on any one thing for a very long time. I always get interested in something else. But you...you are so focused. I admire that. I don't have a passion for anything on Earth like you have for jumping horses. I've never wanted to be anything the way you want to be on that Olympic team. You work hard, all day, every day. It's impressive. I'm a little jealous."

"Really?" She felt a warmth flow into her cheeks.

"Well, what about vet school? That's going to be your career, isn't it? You're going after that, right?"

He shrugged. "I'll finish by summer, but I don't know about being a regular vet. I don't think having a regular clinic feels right."

"You don't know if it feels right? Isn't that a lot of school and time invested not to use the knowledge afterwards? And you're so great with horses."

"Thanks. But that's not what I mean…."

She glanced over at him.

"I want to do some kind of ministry," he said. "So far, that's been going where the Lord leads me and meeting lots of people. I want it to be my work somehow. I want to watch the Lord change people's lives."

"Ha. People like me?" she teased.

"I've never met anyone like you," he said.

"Maybe you need to get out more."

Derrick didn't comment.

She cut her eyes at him and for once he actually looked serious. Emilie cleared her throat. "So, what kind of ministry? Your parents are missionaries in San Salvador, right? Do you want to do something like that?"

"I have no idea." He stretched his arms across the back of the seats. "But I'm not worried. One day,

God will reveal His purpose to me and then I'll be like you, Emilie. Nothing will stop me."

She sighed heavily. "I feel like everything's stopping me. I wish I had your confidence."

"Emilie, if you're not confident then I don't know who is. Anyway, what I've got—it's not confidence. It's a peace and it comes from the Lord. You can have it, too. You just have to ask for it."

"I did, Derrick. I pleaded with God to save my mother. But He didn't. She died of internal injuries two days after her car accident. Then I prayed that I would understand why. But I don't. After that, Karin, my sister, prayed for me to have peace and to know God. And still I felt nothing. Nothing. God doesn't work for me."

Derrick's eyes caressed her with kindness. She could almost feel it. "Sometimes change and understanding don't come when we expect them. But, Emilie, if our hearts aren't open then we won't know the blessings when they do come. And they will come."

Emilie felt a striking pain in her chest. "I don't know. I don't think God has any blessings for me."

"And I know that He does. Trust me. Trust Him. If you believe, the peace will come."

Emilie looked at the dash and swallowed the lump forming in her throat. "I think the defroster quit working."

The defroster? He guessed that not-so-subtle change in subject meant she was finished talking about God. It was a start though. At least she had opened up a little.

Derrick reached for the climate panel on the dash but his eyes stayed on a nearby compact car having a terrible time in the snow. His fingers brushed Emilie's cold hand. With a jerk, she retreated to the steering wheel.

Like at the service, he resisted the urge to grab her hand, hold it and warm it in his own. He shook his head—*ridiculous*—and adjusted the control. A blast of air shot up from the top of the dash and began to clear the frost that had settled on the windshield. Emilie didn't speak.

"So, what else got you so worked up this morning that you were willing to drive off in this storm all alone?"

"How do you know there's something else?"

"A hunch."

"It was Detective Steele."

"Now there's a man with no peace in his heart," he said. "So, what news did he have?"

"Some forensic specialists in D.C. have decided that the killing blow to Camillo had to have been delivered by someone over five foot seven."

"That's great. Then you're no longer a suspect, right?"

"Steele wouldn't admit to that. He said I could have been standing on something and suggested I had an accomplice."

"He just wants to rattle you."

"He does. Why do you think he keeps insisting it's me?"

"I don't know for sure, but he probably thinks you know something else and this is his way to get it from you." He turned to her. "But, you know, his information gives us something else to think about. We could list all the people coming and going from the stable who are over five seven."

"That's almost everyone except for the kids that take lessons, Mrs. Kecksin, Susan and me."

"Perhaps we could even narrow that down to just the men," Derrick said. "Women are rarely killers. That's a statistical fact. And lifting a jump rail requires a lot of upper body strength that most women don't have."

"There are not many men at the stable. The work hands and Gabe, Stephan. Then there are James Joyner, Brent Walker, Mr. Huss, Mr. Adams, my dad, Robert Kramar and you."

"Who's Mr. Huss?"

"The grounds manager of the estate."

"And Kramar?"

"He owns that fabulous gray mare," Emilie said. "The one named Lilly."

"Right. I haven't met him yet. Do Mr. Adams and your dad come to the barn?"

"Hardly ever. And they were both at a dinner the night Camillo died." She shook her head. "I'm sorry, Derrick. I know you're trying to help but it's just silly to think one of those people killed Camillo. Seems crazy to even say such a thing. Camillo got along with everyone. What possible reason could any of those people have to kill him?"

Derrick blew out a long sigh, thinking about her father. "People surprise you sometimes."

"Camillo did. I would never have thought him to keep a secret from me," she said. "And you know what? I still think he had a girlfriend, despite what Lucas said. Despite your strength theory, I don't think we should rule out women."

"What makes you say that?"

"I found a letter. Well, part of a letter. It was in a Bible Camillo gave me for my birthday. He must have forgotten it was in there."

"Like a love letter?"

"More like a Dear John. I found it the day after he died. It was the first time I'd picked up the Bible. Too bad, maybe if I had seen the note earlier, Camillo would have told me what was going on."

"How do you know the message wasn't to you? If it was in the Bible and the Bible was a gift to you?"

"Because Camillo shared a secret with this person—just like you suspected after talking to Lucas. And I know he didn't share any secrets with me."

"Did you show the letter to the police?"

She lifted her chin in the air. "I showed it to Mr. Adams. He was afraid it wouldn't look so good for me. I don't know what he did with it."

Derrick frowned, thinking again of James's words

about Mr. Gill and a cover-up. But why cover up someone who was innocent? "Any idea who his girlfriend could have been? Someone tall, maybe? There's a lot of women at your stable. Lots of tall women."

Emilie glanced at him. "I don't remember Camillo having a preference for tall women, but it sounds like you do."

"Uh…" His checks grew warm. *Actually, I like tiny, green-eyed blondes.* "Not at all. I just thought we were looking for someone over five seven."

"Whatever. Can we just talk about something else?"

"Absolut—" The compact car Derrick had watched struggling in the snow suddenly swerved into their lane. He leaned over and helped Emilie as she fought to keep control of the truck. But she turned the wheel against the slide. Derrick overpowered her, forcing the wheel right, the same direction they were sliding. Carefully, she veered into the emergency lane and applied the brakes. The truck seemed to grip, but the heavy trailer continued to slide across the frozen ground to the right.

"The trailer brake must be frozen. It's not catching."

They slid further and further until the trailer met with the guardrail. Derrick cringed at the sound of the metals colliding.

"The horses!" she cried.

When the wretched sounds died and everything

stopped moving, Derrick jumped out of the truck. Emilie reached for her door handle too.

"No. Stay here," he told her.

She looked ready to argue, but his stern expression must have squashed the coming protest. She gave a weak nod.

Derrick ran behind the trailer. The back door had been badly damaged on the right side. He couldn't open it. He hopped over the guardrail to the side door. It opened enough for him to squeeze in next to Chelsea. The mare pulled hard on her lead. The quick release knot came undone and she charged at Derrick. The chest guard stopped her forward momentum before she could crush him. Chelsea raised her head and backed up until she hit the back door. Then, frustrated and frightened, she kicked out with such force it shook the entire trailer.

"Calm down, girl." Derrick lifted both arms around her tense neck. He whispered low as he stroked her and inspected the wall of the trailer behind her as best he could. It wasn't like he could take the horses out on the highway and check them over. But even with the limited range of sight from where he stood, he figured he'd be able to detect a major injury. The mare, other than being hyped up, looked fine. The damage to the trailer hadn't gone deep enough to reach her. He retied her lead and fed her some carrots that Emilie kept stashed in a little metal compartment.

Bugs whinnied, but the stallion seemed calmer

than Chelsea. Derrick gave the big gray a pat on the face and looked into his section of the trailer. There was nothing there to cause alarm, so he locked them back in, despite their pleas for freedom, and walked back to examine the crunched door. The damage running along the back quarter panel was low and deep but would not prevent them from moving.

He headed to the driver-side door. Through the window he could see Emilie, her lips trembling, her eyes closed. He opened the door. "They're shaken up, but no injuries."

Emilie closed her eyes. A couple of tears squeezed out. "You can drive now." Her voice sounded weak and broken.

He waited for her to slide to the passenger side then climbed in after her. "Why don't we call Peter and tell him about the weather?"

She shook her head. "He's having the same weather. He would have called if he didn't want us to come."

"It won't hurt to check," Derrick said.

"No. Let's just go. We're closer to him than to home."

"It might take an hour in this snow," he said.

"It will take even longer to get home."

Derrick sighed, wishing he'd never let her leave in the first place, as if he had any influence over her. He put the truck in drive and slowly merged back onto the highway.

An hour later they arrived at Winslow Farms. The

perfectly snow-covered ground, the big red clapboard-style stable and surrounding pasture looked like a fancy Christmas card.

Derrick pulled in front of the stable and they hopped out of the truck. Peter Winslow came out to greet them.

"Were you headed to an exhibition, Miss Gill?" Peter asked.

Derrick looked at Emilie and then back to Peter. "We had an appointment," Derrick said. "I spoke with you yesterday, remember?"

"Well, of course, I remember." Peter shook his head. "But then Miss Gill called back and said she'd changed her mind."

"I didn't call you back," Emilie said.

NINE

"Well, it certainly sounded like you. And the call came from your stable. The message was quite clear that you were no longer interested." Mr. Winslow frowned deeply. "In fact, it sounded as if you'd taken up with another trainer. I'm sorry, Miss Gill, but I'm afraid I have a new client, Jack Frahm. He'll arrive in the morning." He turned to face Derrick. "Bring your horses in. There are several open stalls off the back aisle. You're welcome to stay as long as you need."

A new client? Already? Emilie would have been less shocked to hear her own horses speaking English. Her mouth fell open wide as she watched the trainer retreat into the warmth of his stable. She lifted a hand to her head as dark spots began to dance in her line of vision. She blinked hard and rubbed her eyes, but the strange darkening sensation grew worse.

"You don't look so good. Come here." Derrick took her hand and pulled her out of the wind, into the entrance of the stable. He rested his big hands on her shoulders and lowered his head down so that they were forehead to forehead. "Are you okay?"

Tears gathered in the corners of her eyes. "No. I'm not. I don't understand this. Are you sure you didn't call him?"

"Of course I'm sure. Why would I do that?" Derrick stroked her hair. "Anyway, no one could ever confuse my voice with yours."

"You think he imagined the second phone call?"

"No, Peter's not senile. Someone's messing with you, Emilie. And I don't like it." Derrick straightened and drew her into his chest. "I'll get this worked out. Don't worry. Peter's a pushover."

Emilie stiffened. She couldn't remember the last time someone besides her sister had given her a hug. "How is this going to work out? Mr. Winslow is semiretired. He only takes one client per season. And now he's with Jack." She uttered his name with disgust.

"Who's this Jack? I take it you don't think much of him."

"My rotten nemesis."

Derrick kept her in his arms but pulled back and she lifted her head up. His lopsided smile and single dimple made her relax slightly. "Okay. First things first. Let me try to get the doors of the trailer open and get the horses out. After that, I'll talk to Peter."

She sucked in her bottom lip. "I don't think I can

take much more. I keep thinking nothing else could go wrong and then it does. I need Mr. Winslow. For Chelsea." Her body shivered hard and he tightened his hold on her. She dropped her head down and let it settle on the soft fleece of his jacket. "You really wouldn't mind talking to him for me?"

He put his chin on the top of her head. "I'd be glad to. You deserve a decent chance. Things will get better. You'll see."

She lifted a hand to his chest and nodded her head against him.

He pulled away slowly.

She wiped her eyes with the back of her sleeve. "What did you mean exactly when you said 'try to get' the trailer doors open?"

"Oh." Derrick's smile fell. "Here. Come see."

She followed him behind the trailer. The sight of the crushed metal made her stomach weak. Blood drained from her head. "You said everything was okay."

"I said the horses are fine and they are. There was no reason for you to see this before now."

She glared at him.

"I'm going to have to take the doors off the hinges to get them out," he continued. "And I don't even want to think about getting them back into another trailer to get home. I doubt they'll be too fond of traveling for a while. We're gonna have to spend the night." He rubbed his forehead. She wondered if his head hurt as badly as hers. "Peter will help me with this. Go inside the cabin and get warm. You're shivering."

"But I should—"

"Go inside." His voice sounded sharp. "You're too upset to help. Look at you. You're shaking from head to toe. You'd make the horses more nervous than they already are. Anyway, it will give me a chance to speak to Peter."

"Okay." She gave him a quick nod.

Derrick walked into the stable. Emilie fetched her bag from the cab of the truck. But she didn't go straight to the house. Instead, she walked back and stared again at the damage to the trailer. They had been fortunate. It could have been much worse.

She opened the side door and stepped in with her horses. They greeted her with the whites of their eyes and expressed their displeasure at being confined with loud whinnies. As she stroked their faces, they calmed. Chelsea nuzzled her. The loving gesture filled Emilie with shame. Her decision to travel in the snow could have killed them. She leaned against Chelsea's neck, glancing at the back of the trailer. The jagged metal ended less than a foot from her back legs. What if the crash had been worse? If Derrick hadn't grabbed the wheel? If that guardrail hadn't been there? When she closed her eyes, images of the trailer overturning played out in her mind. It had been so stupid of her to leave the farm with the threat of bad weather. She shook her head at the depth of her own selfishness.

"What was I thinking?" Emotion shook her body.

Chelsea rubbed Emilie hard with her big head, almost pushing her from the trailer. "I don't blame you, girl. I deserve that."

Emilie swallowed hard and backed out of the trailer. As she pressed the door closed, her forehead came to rest against it. *I don't blame you one bit. I don't like myself much either.*

When she thought about how badly she'd acted, she wondered why Derrick had even offered to help. And why Camillo had always been so good to her.

A sharp pain ripped through her chest. She readjusted the bag on her shoulder and walked toward the cabin. If how she'd acted this morning was any indication of her true person, she did not like who she'd become. And she feared Derrick was wrong about her and God. Nothing would change. It never did.

Derrick worked with Peter for forty minutes before they got one side of the trailer doors unhinged. With great care, they backed Bugs out of the trailer and took him to a large stall.

Then, by removing the middle divider, Derrick was able to release Chelsea from her little prison.

Peter took the worked-up mare to a small indoor pen where she could stretch her legs. Derrick unpacked the rest of the trailer and checked on the mare again. She trotted nervously to him at the gate. He gave her a peppermint from his pocket.

Poor thing. He rubbed her soft muzzle.

And poor Emilie. He'd never seen anyone look so confused and disappointed.

Lord, thank You for keeping Your hand on us today and for guiding us to safety. Please be with Emilie. Show her Your love....

And maybe make her not smell so good.

Had he been wrong to give her a hug of encouragement? Or just wrong to have enjoyed it so much? Derrick leaned closer to Chelsea and inhaled, hoping the smell of horse would help him forget Emilie's provoking scent. Hoping he could forget how when she'd put her hand on his chest and pressed her head against him, his heart had pounded like he'd run a marathon. Thank goodness she'd gone into the house without fighting. Two more minutes alone and he'd have been dipping his head down to search for those peachy lips. He'd realized yesterday that he was attracted to her, but today it sunk in just how much.

Emilie's a beautiful woman, Lord. I know You don't expect me not to notice that. But do You want me to feel so tender toward her?

Derrick sighed. Falling for Emilie was idiotic for so many reasons. First of all, she didn't share his fervor for the Lord. Number two, she was his boss. Three, she was used to a lifestyle he could never provide. And four, her father...

Lord, make me strong. Help me to be the friend she needs, not a fool. You know my heart and You know I want a wife. I'm lonely. But help me to wait for the right woman.

Derrick sighed. He'd tried to be patient. Over the past few years, he'd passed over many attractive women that didn't share his beliefs without much of a thought. But something inside his heart was stirring now. Something strong. He touched his hand to his chest where he felt it most.

Peter walked up behind him. "I've got a trailer you can use to get home tomorrow. It's supposed to warm up in the morning and melt all the snow."

Derrick turned and nodded.

"We should go in," Peter said. "Think about getting something to eat."

"Could I talk to you for a moment first?" Derrick asked.

"Certainly." Peter leaned against the fence post.

"I know you took on this other rider, but can you at least watch her ride? She really wants to work with you. I know she didn't make that call. She wanted to come here. She wants to work with you. Even the snow wouldn't stop her."

Peter turned his gaze to Chelsea. The mahogany-colored horse sidled over and gave him a sniff. "You think she's worth it?"

Boy, was Peter asking the wrong person. "I don't know the show circuit. But I know people and there's no way anyone wants to be the best more than she does."

Peter scratched his head. "I don't like working with two riders in the same circuit. Conflict of interest. And I'm semiretired, you know."

"But watch her. Just once. Anything. She's had a bad week. Come on, Peter. I can't go back in there with nothing."

Peter lifted a brow. "How about this? I'll watch her in the morning and if she does well, she can stay with Jack for the week. I'll make my decision then. I suppose I could manage two riders for that long."

Derrick reached out and shook Peter's hand vigorously. "Thank you. I'm really grateful. I'll go tell her."

"Let's go in and have some tea, eh?" Peter smiled.

The two men headed out of the stable, passing by the truck and wrecked trailer.

"What's that?" Peter pointed to something dark and frayed hanging to the ground beneath the hitch.

Derrick squatted, reaching under the vehicle. His fingers wrapped around the loose item and pulled it into the light. His gloved opened, exposing a wad of cut wires.

"Good gracious," Peter gasped. "The entire brake line has been severed. Could that have happened during the accident?"

Derrick stood, staring at the mass in his hand. "I

don't think so. My guess is this was done before. It's why Emilie couldn't get the trailer to stop skidding. We thought the brakes had frozen up. Looks like they weren't even connected." He looked up at Peter. "And looks like someone's interested in killing more than Emilie's groom."

TEN

Derrick drove the salt-streaked highways back to Cedar Oaks alone the next day. The sun blazed over central Virginia. Hardly a trace of snow was left by midday, and by then, Emilie had earned at least a week with Peter. The drive back seemed longer than the previous day's trip through the snow. All because he missed Emilie and he knew that he shouldn't.

He wouldn't see her again until the first winter show at the end of the week. And that was for the best. He and Peter both agreed she could use a change of scenery. Not to mention, she might be safer away from her own stable. At least, he hoped she would be. Maybe the case would be solved before she returned. Anything was possible. In the meantime, he'd meet with Detective Steele and discuss the cut brake line.

Derrick pulled the broken trailer back to the stable. Detective Steele's nondescript sedan awaited him at the front doors. Derrick showed him the cut wires, which he placed in an evidence bag. Then the detective called a colleague to come take a look at the undercarriage and at her other vehicles. While they waited, Derrick invited him in for a cup of coffee. He wanted one himself.

He unlocked Emilie's office, flipped the lights on and froze. Filing drawers had been opened and dumped, papers strewn about, the sofa cushions ripped and pictures were broken or hanging askew.

Detective Steele let out a whistle. "Somebody was looking for something in a hurry. Cash, maybe?" He popped on a pair of latex gloves and started to inspect the door lock. "A good pick job or someone had a key." He surveyed the room quickly then turned to Derrick. "Does it look like anything is missing?"

"I wouldn't know. Especially if it was something small or paperwork…Emilie would be the person to ask."

"Will she be back soon?"

"No, she's staying in Warrenton for the week."

"And you said that you left together yesterday morning?"

"Yes. Around seven in the morning."

"The forensic unit is already on the way," Steele said as if he weren't very interested. "Why don't we have a look around the rest of the barn?"

Derrick led the detective through the stable. The place seemed strangely devoid of life.

"Gabe should be here working the afternoon shift. He must be late." Derrick checked a few of the stalls for signs they'd been cleaned that morning. "Stephan was scheduled this morning. Looks like he was here. The stalls are clean and the horses out."

Steele looked around with a casual air. Was he not making the same connection? Did he not think the break-in was related to Garcia's death? Annoyed, Derrick turned the corner into the old stable and stopped. They had interrupted a teenaged couple stealing a kiss.

Derrick cleared his throat loudly. "Hi, Deirdre. Didn't know you were here."

"We were just…uh." Deirdre's face turned red as she shook her short, bleached hair and stared down at the ground.

"No one is supposed to cross the yellow tape." Steele stepped forward with an air of authority.

Derrick motioned toward him. "This is Detective Steele. There's been a break-in at the stable."

"A break-in?" Deirdre gasped.

"Yes. Have you see anybody while you were here?" Steele asked.

She blushed. "I…um…didn't really notice."

"I'll escort these two out and check back here." Steele glared at the young couple.

Derrick made his way to the feed room and prepared the horses' dinner. His thoughts stuck on the ransacked office. As he measured out their feed, he noticed that a white powder dusted the countertops and some of the medicines were out of place. He grabbed the feed supplements for Duchess and opened the can. A bitter odor flowed out of the container instead of the usual sweet aroma of vitamins and electrolytes. He looked inside the mixture. Something had been added, making the normally brown substance look grayish.

Derrick shuddered and looked around the room full of medicines. How many others of them had been tainted?

He closed the lid, shutting in the bitter smell, and went to find Detective Steele.

"Let go of her head," Mr. Winslow yelled.

"I thought I did," Emilie mumbled under her breath and cut her eyes at the trainer. Then she slowed the young paint to a walk.

Winslow marched across the sand-filled indoor ring and summoned her to meet him in the center. He grabbed her hands and lifted them halfway up the horse's mane. "You are here." He stretched her hands to the horse's ears, pulling her entire body out of the saddle. "When you start over the fence, I want you here."

He was kidding, right? Her small frame could hardly reach that far. No way she could stretch like that and maintain a firm leg. She blew out a heavy sigh and sat back in the saddle.

Dropping her reins, she glared up at the metal ceiling. All this criticism was starting to get to her. Had she done anything right? She knew that she had. She'd ridden well the entire week, but Mr. Winslow still found things to criticize.

Jack Frahm trotted by on his gray gelding, ready for his turn over the triple combination. He'd been there all week training right alongside of her, reminding her of college when they'd ridden for the same team. Only now he was no longer her boyfriend and teammate. He was the competition.

"Watch and learn, Emilie," Jack goaded, as he passed by. "Watch and learn."

She clenched her teeth and cleared the ring, walking her horse along the outside of the fence. It was past time for dinner but Mr. Winslow had not dismissed her. Probably waiting to point out something else she did wrong.

Jack took his trip over the combination. His gray mare popped over the three jumps like a gazelle. Emilie groaned. Jack's riding had improved. Considerably. And he made every effort to vex her over it, making the week with him both miserable and eye-opening. How had she not seen Jack's true character before? He was such a cad—one minute he'd charm and the next he'd insult, and always with that same cheesy smirk on his face. She thought of Derrick's genuine smile. How false Jack's seemed in comparison. What had she ever seen in him?

Her chest tightened. She looked down and fiddled with her reins. It wasn't a question to ponder. She knew the answer. She'd seen herself in Jack. Or something close to it. Strange how his attitude disgusted her now. Was it possible she had changed? The idea lit a small flame of hope within her.

"Miss Gill, once more through the combo." Mr. Winslow waved her back into the ring. Jack rode off, dismounted and led his horse from the arena.

Emilie trotted to Mr. Winslow in the center of the ring and halted. "Is there anything you like about my riding?"

The trainer made a strange face. "You're a fine equestrian, Miss Gill. One of the best in the world. You don't need me to tell you that."

"Then why do I need to change so many things?"

"Because you have no trust, Miss Gill. You need trust. Change will help you learn that. You'll see."

"But…" *Trust what? Change what?* Was he talking about her life or her riding?

The trainer brushed imaginary dust from his hunter green Ralph Lauren sweater. "Do you have another question, Miss Gill?"

She shook her head. "No."

"Then, let's see that triple."

Emilie closed her eyes and cleared her head of everything except the three jumps in the center of the ring and Mr. Winslow's words. Her fingers tightened around the reins and her heel tapped the horse. They cantered in a wide circle.

Trust. The concept made her pulse spike. The horse pulled and yanked the reins with every stride. Emilie fought for control. *Trust.* Trust this crazy horse? The mare sidestepped. Great. Now they were crooked to the approach. *Trust.* Emilie fought the urge to tug on the horse's mouth. Instead, she lifted her hands, moved up the horse's neck and gave up control. A huge loop in the leather reins formed below the mare's neck. The timing was wrong. The mare took off late, shaking her head at freedom. And it didn't matter.

They cleared all three jumps with room to spare.

The trainer called her over, his smile displaying every one of his tea-stained teeth. "That was trust, Miss Gill. How did it feel?"

"Different." She halted in front of him and caught her breath. "Different. But okay."

"You trusted her. Well done."

Well done. Her chest filled with air. "Thank you, sir."

The trainer eyed her for a moment. "I'm going to a Bible study tonight. I'd like very much if you would join me."

Bible study? With Mr. Winslow? Her eyes grew wider. "I—uh…"

The cell phone at her waist pulsed. She dismounted and pulled the phone from its clip—ever since Derrick had told her about the break-in and the trailer brakes, she'd kept it glued to her body, even during practice. She bit her lip as she read the caller ID. "It's Derrick. Hopefully not more bad news."

Mr. Winslow nodded. He took the reins from her and led the horse into the stable, leaving her alone in the indoor ring.

"Everything okay?" she asked as she answered the call.

"Oh, yeah. Holding down the fort. How about you? You surviving?" Derrick said.

Emilie smiled at the sound of his voice. "I'm doing well for being in equestrian boot camp."

He chuckled. "That bad?"

"An hour ago I was about to ring the bell."

"What? You? Give up? I can't believe that."

Emilie unlatched her riding helmet and stuck it under her arm. "Believe it."

"Can I do anything to help?"

Tell me again how you admire me. She pictured his warm smile. "Actually, I just got my first compliment."

"Wow. One whole compliment." His playfulness made her laugh. "Don't let it go to your head."

"And Mr. Winslow invited me to a Bible study."

"No kidding. You gonna go?"

"Of course not."

"Why not? I thought you'd agreed to keep your mind open."

She thought about the trust and change that Mr. Winslow and Derrick had spoken to her about. "I didn't agree to anything. That was just you talking."

He laughed. "I think you should go. In fact, I'll make you a deal—I'll ride a real Grand Prix course of your choosing if you go to the Bible study."

"Have you ever jumped that high before?"

"Nope."

"Now that could be interesting." She smiled, considering his proposal.

"So, how's your rival?"

"Jack? Ugh. Don't remind me. It was nice to not think about him for five seconds."

"So the competition has gotten better, huh?" Derrick asked.

"I don't get it. The guy can do no wrong."

"Emilie." His deep voice sounded soft. "It doesn't matter what he does there. If he can't do it in the show ring then it means nothing."

His words felt like a warm hug around her heart. She pressed the phone tightly to her cheek. "You're right. What we do here doesn't matter. Thanks for reminding me," she said. "Now what's the bad news?"

Derrick paused. "How do you know I have bad news?"

"You only call when there's bad news."

"Then I guess I need to call more often."

Emilie's heart skipped a beat even though she knew he teased her.

"Well, first the good news. With all the events happening while you were away, Steele hasn't accused you of any of them."

"Very funny," she said. "What did he really say?"

"He can't do anything about the cut brakes. The wires were handled by too many people. And since you haven't used that particular trailer in months, there was no way to know when they were cut. He suggested putting an alarm on the trailer barn."

"Okay."

"In the office, I don't think anything is missing. Although I'm not familiar with it like you are. So maybe you'll see something I missed. Steele suspects it was teenagers looking for cash."

"I guess that is possible, but how did they get in?"

"Well, that's the problem with the story. His guess is they got lucky picking the lock. He thinks we should change all the locks."

"Sure. Go ahead."

"I did. I called a security expert. He'll be out next week," Derrick said. "Emilie, I also told Steele about the phony phone call to Peter. He said he'd look into it. But since anyone can walk into the stable and use the phone, he didn't have a lot of hope."

"So, no real answers, huh?"

"No, but here's the really bad news…in the feed room, the police took samples from every container and the results came back today. Someone spiked the supplements for your horses with extra protein and amphetamines."

"Just my horses?"

"Yes."

"That could have killed them."

"Or you."

The phone trembled in Emilie's hand. "Why? Why would anyone do that? *Who* would do that? Jack?"

"Yes, maybe a competitor. Seems likely that the phone call to Peter was from a competitor, too. But not necessarily Jack. I've been thinking about what you said about it being a woman. What female competitors would come to mind?"

"I don't know. Leslie Raney. Joan Stipes. Deborah Long. But what are you saying? You think all this is related? Like someone is trying to keep me off the Olympic team?"

"Seems like it to me," he said.

"What about Camillo? How would he fit into that?"

"Something to do with his secret, maybe? If someone was trying to hurt you, and Camillo got in the way, trying to protect you… But face it, Emilie. Someone *is* targeting you."

"You're the only one thinking that, Derrick."

"I'm the only one who knows what it's like to be your groom."

There was a strange silence between them and suddenly Emilie felt as though Derrick, too, were keeping a secret from her.

ELEVEN

Derrick closed up the stable, showered and rang the front bell to the Gill manse. Rosa, the housekeeper, opened the door.

"Mr. Gill is in the bar." She pointed to a door on the left.

Derrick swallowed hard, his fingers tight on the packet of money he'd found in the fridge. He rounded the corner. Mr. Gill sat perched on a tall leather stool, drink in hand, watching stock exchange updates on a plasma screen fixed to the wall above.

"Come in, Randall." Mr. Gill loosened the square-knotted tie.

Derrick walked inside the small but manly space. The bar was solid mahogany floor to ceiling, with a billiards table to the front and three card tables between. The walls were dark green and the floor cherry. Hunting scenes hung on the walls. The faint smell of cigar smoke lingered in the air.

"I've heard nothing but good so far," he said. "Not one complaint from my daughter."

His words slurred and Derrick could now see the glassed-over look in his eyes.

"How about a drink?"

"No. Thank you. I just came to return this." Derrick handed him the packet of money. "I believe this belongs to you."

Mr. Gill snatched the envelope from his hands and tossed it on the bar. "Okay, fine. You win. No bonus. If that's the way you want to play it."

"Yes, sir. I don't feel right about it," Derrick said. "Thank you for understanding. Good night." Derrick started out of the room, wondering if Mr. Gill would even remember this conversation in the morning.

"Carolyn never understood the things I did, either," Mr. Gill said. "You know, they look just alike."

Derrick stopped at the door and turned back. "Sir?"

Mr. Gill's eyes glistened. "Emilie's mother. Carolyn. Guess I'm missing her tonight." He grabbed a nearby remote and turned off the television.

"Should I call the housekeeper, sir? You look tired."

"She left the house so angry," he continued, shaking his head and ignoring Derrick's question. "You'll never guess what we were arguing about."

Derrick shifted his weight and glanced down the hallway, looking for Rosa.

"Emilie, of course," Mr. Gill said. "Carolyn was worried about her traveling with Camillo. Didn't think I had the situation taken care of. She'd heard things about him. Some of it was probably true, I suppose. But she didn't know what I knew. I should have..." His words trailed off and he took a long drink from the old-fashioned.

"How about I get you some water, sir?" Derrick moved behind the bar and searched for a glass.

Mr. Gill leaned over the bar in his direction. "Now Emilie is upset about the investigation on Camillo." He snorted. "Ironic, isn't it? She doesn't think I can take care of things, either. She has no idea the lengths I go to to protect her."

Derrick poured a glass of water for Mr. Gill and slid it across the bar. The man nodded his thanks.

He picked up the glass and gave Derrick an icy stare. "Just remember this, Randall. You work here. You work for me. Whether you take the tips or not." He stood and staggered out of the room.

The Bible study consisted of five elderly men and two women who'd all but smothered Emilie with unwanted hugs and pats. And then when they prayed, she felt strangely alone. The verse they'd studied had planted itself into her brain. "Those who know Your name will trust You, for You, Lord, have never forsaken those who seek You." Emilie thought of Derrick's and Mr. Winslow's words. Could she trust the Lord? Could she change? Did she need to know Camillo's secret for that to happen? Her mind was stuck on thoughts of all that had happened over the past week. Then she thought of Pastor Lucas, of his warning and his news about Camillo.

Camillo was afraid. He'd planned to go to California.

California? Camillo had lived there before coming to Virginia. Perhaps he still had contacts there. A subtle smile fixed over Emilie's lips as she thought of Sam Prior, the Californian ranch owner who also brokered high-end stable help.

When Emilie returned to Winslow Farms, she grabbed her cell phone and dialed information.

"City, please."

"Indigo Desert, California."

"Listing, please."

"Triple M Ranch."

"One moment, please."

Within seconds, the automated operator connected her.

"Sam Prior, Triple M."

Wow. Too easy. "Sam. This is Emilie Gill. I'm calling about—"

"Little Emilie! How are you? I heard you're training with Winslow."

"Yes—"

"How's that going? I heard he's getting senile. Is that true?"

"No. I don't—"

"I helped that groom of yours out with a new job. But what happened to him? The guy never showed up. Did you give him a counteroffer?"

"You placed Camillo?" Her palms grew sweaty as she gripped the phone more tightly.

"Not exactly. You know I have to have current references and he said he couldn't provide them. So, I told him to call Mike Evans, you know, that buddy of mine who owns Del Santos. He needed some seasonal help. Garcia said that sounded even better. As far as I know, he was supposed to get here around Thanksgiving. But he never showed up."

Emilie dropped her head. "He was murdered."

"Are you serious?" A few expletives sounded on the other end of the line.

"Sam, did Camillo tell you why he was leaving and coming out to California?"

"Not really. But I didn't ask. I just assumed things weren't working out between you and him. You know, the way he was saying how you wouldn't give him a reference and all. He did ask me not to call you. Said he hadn't told you he was leaving yet."

"What about your friend Mike? Didn't he want a reference?"

"Not Mike. He pays cash. Probably has a few illegals working for him."

"Thanks, Sam. If your friend Mike knows anything, could you have him call me?"

"Will do. You take care now."

"You, too." She dropped the phone into her lap, her hands shaking. Since when did Camillo need to take seasonal work? And since when would she not give him a reference? That was a total lie.

Did he just not want her to know he was leaving? Or was there more to it than that?

TWELVE

"What do you mean you're only going to work with one of us?" Jack Frahm shifted his lanky figure and glared down at Mr. Winslow.

Emilie shrank between the two men, wishing the trainer had picked a different spot to make his announcement. The middle of New Gate's gigantic indoor arena buzzed with riders, spectators, vendors, not to mention the Outdoor Sports Channel crew and cameras. It wasn't exactly private. Even with the jumbo screen playing videos and speakers jamming rock tunes between riders, Jack's raised voice drew attention from the milling crowds and the enormous queue for coffee that wrapped around the walkway where they stood.

Emilie dipped her head. If she wanted to be noticed, it would be for riding, not for making a public scene. She peeled the black leather gloves from her sweaty fingers and said nothing. Winslow's announcement didn't exactly surprise her. In a way, it brought relief. No way could she take another week of Jack Frahm.

Mr. Winslow stepped closer. He glanced at her, then his small brown eyes darted up to Jack. "It's a conflict of interest to work with both of you. But, I didn't want to leave anyone out in the cold. No one will be without a trainer for the Winter Series. Katherine Ellis will take one of you. As you know, she's quite competent. I was hoping the two of you might decide between yourselves how to proceed. If not, my decision is to work with today's winner." With his lips pressed flat, he nodded to them both and moved off toward the pastry stand.

Jack groaned. "Ellis? I don't want to work with Ellis." He shoved his riding helmet under one arm and stared at Emilie. She expected steam to come flying out of his ears at any moment.

"I don't particularly care to work with Ellis either. I did a clinic with her once." Emilie remembered the woman had done nothing but praise her every move. Even though that might be a pleasant change from Mr. Winslow's constant corrections, it was not what she needed at this point in her career. "Let's just do what he said. Today's show can decide. You finish higher, you work with Winslow. I finish higher, I get him."

"Fine with me." With an exaggerated movement, Jack swept his fingers through his sandy-colored hair, turned on his heels and marched off toward the trailers.

Good riddance. Emilie sighed.

"Miss Gill! Miss Gill!"

Over her shoulder, she saw the Outdoor Sports Channel cameraman and reporter busting through the coffee line to get to her. She thought about dodging them behind the leather goods booth next door, but before she could move, a strong hand gripped her by the elbow and pulled her in another direction.

"Here." Derrick handed her a bottle of water. "I'll get rid of them."

She took the water as Derrick turned and faced the reporter, using his body as a buffer between her and the two-man TV crew.

"Miss Gill, is it true you were arrested for killing your own groo—" The reporter was forced to stop in front of Derrick's large frame. "Could you step aside? You're blocking the shot."

Derrick smiled but didn't budge. "Miss Gill will have an interview after the Grand Prix competition."

"What are you? Her private bodyguard?" the reporter asked with an annoyed tone.

Others crowded around trying to get the attention of the cameraman so that they could be on television. Derrick took a step back, letting the people fill in the space where he'd been. He and Emilie escaped. He guided her to an empty corner beside center ring.

"Thanks." She popped the chin strap from her helmet and took a long drink, finishing the cold beverage in a few gulps.

Derrick shook his dark hair and wiped the gleaming sweat from his forehead. "You'll probably have to talk to them later."

She lifted her eyebrows and sighed. "Yeah. Mr. Adams told me what to say, but I kind of liked dodging them like that. That was more fun than being diplomatic."

Derrick looked down and reciprocated the grin on her face.

"Speaking of the case, any new developments?" she asked. "More and more I'm thinking it had to be Frahm. He's such a slime. I think he'd do anything to get on that Olympic team."

Derrick paused. "You sure you want to talk about this now?"

"Why not? It's always on my mind."

"Okay. Well, Steele was out to the stable yesterday. He said there's nothing linking the events together. He thinks it could have been vandals, or teenagers… just your everyday barn theft gone wrong. But you know how I feel about that."

"How could he think that about the amphetamines?"

"Exactly. He called that a terrible prank."

She cut her eyes up at him. "What can we do?"

"While you were gone, I got the names of the folks in the Bible study and talked to them. Turns out, they all had ties to the stable. Mrs. Kecksin, Robert Kramar and Tiffany Collier."

"Tiffany? The new weekend stable hand? You

know, Camillo hired her. You think she was his love interest?"

"No." Derrick tilted his head. "I thought the same thing, especially after talking to her. It's obvious she had been interested. But according to Mrs. Kecksin, Camillo never reciprocated her feelings. What I did learn was that all of them found Camillo, during his last week or two, to be extremely nervous and unusually quiet. Also, Mrs. Kecksin gave me a business card from a friend of Camillo's. Hector Emens, he did some landscaping for Mr. Kecksin. I called him and he said he'd meet with us when we get back from the show. Mrs. Kecksin said Hector and Camillo were good friends and seemed to think Hector might know more than the Bible study group."

Emilie took a deep breath. "That sounds good. You know, I found out where Camillo was headed."

"Really?" Derrick looked her square in the eye.

"Yes, I called a friend of mine who brokers out high-end grooms and stable help in California. Camillo had arranged for some seasonal work through him."

Derrick shook his head. "But I don't get that. Why would Camillo do that kind of work when he could run a barn?"

"Exactly." She put a hand on her hip. "Camillo told my friend that I wouldn't give him a reference."

"And that's not true?"

"Of course not."

"Well, I guess that was part of his keeping it all secret," Derrick said.

She shrugged. "I guess."

"Emilie, I know this is on your mind, but right now let's get you through this show. I want you focused. One hundred percent focused on the ride. Nothing else."

Emilie turned her attention to the main ring. A delicate, dun-colored thoroughbred tore through the difficult amateur course, churning up a wake of sand as the rider spurred her on too quickly. Derrick put a hand on her shoulder. She looked up and studied his face. "You knew about Winslow's decision, didn't you?"

Derrick ran his other hand through his mussed-up hair. "I kind of guessed he would do something like that—"

"And you didn't warn me?" She looked back at the dun mare.

"If I'd been sure, I would have said something, although I don't see what good it would have done."

"True." She expelled a ragged breath. "So, tell me. Why doesn't Winslow just dump me? I don't think I can beat Jack today."

Derrick lifted her chin to his face and turned her from the ring, lowering his head and shoulders until they were level with hers. "What? What did you say?"

She searched his face. "I don't think I can beat him."

"I know you don't believe that inside. Come on, Emilie. Forget this investigation for a few hours. Focus on today one hundred percent. None of what happened in training matters. You have great horses. Get out there and show them off like only you can do."

His fingers at her neck made her skin tingle. A smile tugged at her lips. "You're right. You're right."

Derrick straightened to full height again. "Of course, I'm right. You can win this, Emilie. I know it in here."

He took her hand and touched it to his chest where his heart would be. Her eyes followed then her gaze lifted back to his face. The intensity of his eyes pulled at her and the connection moved through her right down to her toes, so strong she couldn't swallow.

"How about I grab us some lunch?" Derrick stepped back.

"Oh." She shook her head. "I don't eat before an event. Just after."

"Oh yeah. The dinner you're going to cook."

"That's right. For everyone who helped at the show. That'd be Mr. Winslow and our trailer help, Susan and Brent."

Derrick lifted an eyebrow. "So you're telling me I still haven't managed to get an invite to dinner?"

She smirked.

"In that case, I'd better get some lunch. Meet you at the trailer." Derrick eased the empty water bottle from her fingers and headed off toward the vendors. Her heart beat wildly as she watched him move away until she could no longer distinguish his dark hair from the rest of the crowd.

Derrick touched a hand to Bugs's coat. The horse was cool, but he led the stallion around the practice ring again, anyway. If he left now, he'd miss watching Emilie's ride center ring on Marco. Her last opportunity to beat Frahm.

Derrick's stomach tied in knots so tight he could hardly breathe as his eyes fixed on the jumbo screen above. Emilie had ridden well all day, but Jack was above her in the standings. In fact, Frahm and one other rider had been the only two competitors to go clean in the final jump-off. Emilie had the pressure of not only riding through clean but also beating Jack's time of seventy-four seconds. Fortunately, she had the advantage of being the last rider.

He knew she worried about Marco and the water jump. The gelding had barely cleared it in the preliminary round, and for the jump-off, the approach was more difficult.

Derrick bit his lower lip, watching Emilie take her opening circle. She chose a crooked line to the first jump and he cringed. But they cleared and took the second jump at an angle as well. He raised an eyebrow at her strategy—she was trying to shave off tenths of seconds by cutting the approaches. It was a good plan; it just made his stomach weak. He tightened his fists around Bugs's lead rope. On the big screen, Marco tucked his legs to the side to clear the solid wall. Third, fourth, fifth jumps, all clear, still Derrick couldn't breathe.

Emilie tapped Marco's hip with a crop, urging him on.

Don't go too fast, he said to himself.

He shielded his eyes from the screen. It was torture to watch. It was torture not to watch. His legs shook. They felt like rubber under him. *A bundle of nerves. That's what I am.* So much at stake for Emilie. He wanted so badly for her to stay with Peter. Not just for training, but for guidance and friendship. She needed people in her life who knew the Lord. Derrick lowered his head.

Lord, You know best, but I think Peter is good for Emilie. Your will be done.

Simultaneous gasps sounded from the crowd. His heart fell to his stomach but he forced his head up to see the big screen. Marco had rubbed a rail. The camera zoomed in to show it wobbling in the cup then zoomed back out.

Next jump. Marco's hooves crossing the fifteen-foot long pool of water.

Derrick held his breath again. Emilie galloped on.

The rail did not fall. The hooves did not touch the

water. A close-up of her determined face illuminated the enormous screen above.

Please, Lord.

Last jump. Clean. She crossed the time line. No faults. Seventy-three and two-tenths seconds. Her time blinked in the upper corner of the screen. She wasn't the overall winner but she had beaten Jack.

"Yes!" Derrick let out a whoop. She did it. She'll keep Peter. *Thank You, Lord.*

Derrick ran Bugs to Emilie's trailer then rushed to the center ring to get Marco. During the awards ceremony as Emilie accepted her second-place prize money, Derrick stood beside Peter. And even though the old codger said nothing, Derrick sensed the man was quite pleased with the outcome of the show.

Derrick liked that Emilie smiled a bit on the way home. But as they rolled onto the estate, her spirits plummeted like a meteor. Her shoulders fell. Her expression soured. The break-in, the unsolved murder, the loss of her friend hung about her like a heavy chain. He felt it, too, but not nearly as she must have.

He parked the enormous gooseneck trailer in front of the stable and stepped out. Emilie hesitated in the passenger seat. Derrick left her and walked around to the back doors, pulling on the heavy latches. They clicked open. The horses whinnied, ready to unload, happy to be home. He pulled the ramp out and glanced over at the stable entrance. Emilie stood there motionless.

"I cleaned up the office," he called out. "I didn't want you to see it like that."

She looked at him over her shoulder. "Thanks. I guess I still need to see if anything is missing."

"Not tonight." He dropped the ramp into place and walked toward her. Her cheeks looked the color of ivory under the light of the porch. He wanted to cradle them in his palms. With a deep breath, he leaned back against one of the thick white columns supporting the fancy front porch. "Steele did want you to call after you looked it over…but you can do it tomorrow. Why don't you go on home? You can face all of this tomorrow."

"No. I want to get this over with," she said, staring at the ground.

"Should I go in with you?"

Emilie nodded and turned toward the approaching car. "There's Susan and Brent. Let them unload. You've done enough today."

"I'm not going to argue with you on that." He hoped to make her smile. But instead, he saw tears glistening in the corners of her eyes. His fingers ached to wipe them. His chest constricted. His gaze fell to her pink lips.

Derrick forced his eyes to the ceiling, clenching his teeth as he held the door open for her. He was tired and when he was tired his thoughts wandered where they shouldn't. Wandered on things like kissing peachy lips and touching creamy, soft skin. Things he had no business thinking about. Emilie was his boss and his friend. Neither relationship included giving into the ideas he entertained at the moment.

Derrick followed her to the office then turned to leave.

"No. Stay," she whispered.

He leaned nonchalantly against the doorjamb, his heart racing. She looked around the space, opened drawers and touched things, paused in front of her trophy stand.

"I'm not missing anything obvious. But I'll have to look through the paperwork tomorrow. I'm too tired now." She turned to the center of the room. One finger slipped between her teeth and she bit down on the nail. "I didn't realize how hard it would be to come back."

"I'm sorry. I really don't think you should be dealing with this now. It's been a long day."

Emilie continued to stare at her trophies. "You know, I keep remembering Camillo those last few weeks. Going over and over in my mind all our conversations. There must have been something he said to me to clue me in. To let me know that he was in trouble. I should have sensed it. If I weren't stuck on myself, thinking about winning all the time, none of this would have happened…."

"Don't do that to yourself." Derrick shook his head. "No way any part of this is your fault. Don't do that. Let's get out of here. Face this tomorrow. Tonight, you have something to celebrate. You did great today."

She looked up, her face sad but relaxed. "I went to that Bible study."

"Peter mentioned it." Derrick couldn't keep a smile from his lips.

"Well…" She lifted an eyebrow. "I have a question."

"Questions are good. I ask God questions all the time." *Like, why did He put me in this job? And what should I do with my life?*

"Yes, well, this question is for you."

"Fire away."

"At the Bible study, people were saying that we should love God because He first loved us. Then everyone was talking about how they feel God's love this way or that way. You know, like when they hold a baby or smell a rose. And they were all so overcome with emotion."

He nodded.

"Well." She looked down at the floor. "I've never experienced that. I look at a sunset and I think it's pretty. But just because God made it I don't see how that means He loves me. I think something's wrong with me."

She doesn't feel love? Lord, how can this be? A sharp pain shot through his chest. It took every ounce of his will not to draw her up in his arms. "There's nothing wrong with you, Emilie."

"Do you have those kind of moments?" Her sad look searched his face.

"I do. Sometimes. But there was a time when I didn't."

"What was different?"

"I was confused about some things. But over time I worked through it."

"So it just takes time?" She looked frustrated.

"Yes. And the will to grow close to Him." He leaned forward and took her hand. "Have you ever had a horse that ran from you every time you tried to get him out of a field, that didn't like to be brushed and turned his backside to you when you came to his stall?"

"Sure. Lots of horses are grumpy like that."

"Maybe they're grumpy. Maybe they're scared. Maybe they don't trust you. I think sometimes we treat God like those horses treat us. He's reaching out and we can't feel it. We're not trusting Him and accepting His love."

She narrowed her eyes at him. "You think I'm a grumpy horse?"

"No." He released her hand while he still could. "I think something's keeping you from experiencing God's love. You can figure out what that is and change it."

Emilie rolled her eyes. "How do you make everything sound so simple?"

"I don't mean to." He moistened his lips. "Does that bother you?"

"A lot." Her dark green eyes bore into him. "*You* bother me a lot. You're so *happy* all the time. It's impossible not to be friends with you. And I really didn't want to like you."

"I noticed that," he said. "What changed?" The words croaked out of his suddenly dry mouth.

"Maybe I did. I didn't think it was possible for people to change. But all the things that are happening to me. Around me." She shrugged. "It's making me think about things…." She stopped, smiled then gave him a sideways stare. "You're making a very strange face. What are you thinking?"

"I was thinking that…" *I want to kiss you.* Derrick dropped his head. *Help me out, Lord.* "I was thinking that maybe you used to be a grumpy horse." Derrick gave her a brotherly punch in the shoulder.

"Ha." She grinned. Flecks of yellow shimmered in her dark green eyes. "I'll go find Susan and Brent and get them started."

He let out a deep sigh as she walked away.

"And I suppose you've earned your invite to dinner," her voice sounded from the hallway.

He looked over his shoulder. Her big smile flashed and her eyes sparkled. Did she have any idea how adorable she was?

"Come up to the main house in an hour," she added.

He nodded, thankful that Brent and Susan

would be at her dinner. No chance of crazy, hopeless thoughts getting into his head with those silly kids around.

THIRTEEN

After a long shower and change of clothes, Derrick searched the apartment for a decent pair of shoes to wear down to the main house. He brushed at the wrinkles in his shirt, only to notice even more of them in his slacks. Perhaps he should forget the shoes and hunt for an iron.

An iron. Ha. Since when did he worry about a couple of wrinkles in his shirt? It wasn't as if he was going on a date.

A date. The idea made his pulse spike? Images of Emilie filled his head.

Don't go there, Randall. She's your boss.

Derrick swallowed hard. Yes, Emilie Gill was his boss, but that was a temporary problem and secondary to many others, such as the fact that she didn't share his beliefs or that she was accustomed to riches he could never provide.

Shaking the water from his hair with his fingertips, Derrick located a pair of flip-flops he'd left in front of the couch. He slipped them on and dredged his way to the kitchen. The view from the large picture window made him pause. He wiped a hand across his freshly shaven chin as he admired the beautiful extravagance of the gardens—thousands of twinkling lights, seasonal flowers, perfectly trimmed shrubs, all graced with tasteful fountains and statues. Even in the cold of December, the open space looked inviting. His gaze lifted from the gardens to the kitchen windows of the house. Behind the curtains, he saw movement.

Emilie.

His breath stuck in his throat.

Derrick transferred his focus to the fridge, smiling at the fine array of choices. He spotted a bottle of springwater in the back. Reaching over the milk, his fingers tapped a thick packet.

Not again.

With dread, he pulled the envelope from the shelf and looked inside. More cash. Derrick groaned.

"I don't want this money," he grumbled to no one. How many times did he have to tell this man? Apparently once more.

The gold-trimmed Escalade had been parked outside the front of the home. Most likely, Mr. Gill was there. Why not talk to him right now? He was headed over there anyway.

Derrick took the new envelope of cash and started for the door. Maybe tonight he could finally explain to Mr. Gill how his actions were hurting Emilie instead of protecting her. And tell him how if he didn't confess to Emilie about his arrangement with Camillo, that he planned to do it himself.

Derrick yanked his coat from a chair back and headed out into the crisp night air.

"Here, Brent." Emilie handed the lanky teenaged boy a ziplock bag. "When you get home, put the fish on some foil and reheat it in your toaster oven."

"Wow. Thanks. Sorry I have to go. Got homework to do."

"No problem." Emilie grinned. "Thanks for helping out. And I forgot to tell you guys, when I place, everyone gets a little bonus check. I'll have it for you next weekend."

"Sweet!" Brent did a fist pump as he walked through the double front doors. He glanced back at Susan. "Hey Suz, do you—"

"Bye, Brent. See you next weekend." The girl raced forward practically closing the door in his face.

Emilie lifted a brow. "What was that about?"

"Nothing." Susan lifted her head and strutted back to the kitchen.

Emilie followed, watching the girl's short brown bob swing back and forth with each quick step. Seemed like she'd had that same haircut since kindergarten, or whenever it was she'd started riding at Cedar Oaks. On the other hand, the rest of Susan had changed during the last year. She was no little girl anymore. Perhaps Brent had noticed. Emilie bit her lip to keep from laughing. "So, Brent likes you."

"I guess. He asked if I would go with him to his school's Christmas dance." Susan's body language said she didn't care, but her face had turned fire-engine red. "He wants me to answer him right now. I don't know what to say."

Emilie nodded as she piled four dinner plates with salmon steaks and covered them with her mango salsa. "Well, I haven't dated a whole lot. But I think yes or no usually works."

"Come on." The girl tilted her head sideways. "Of course, I would say yes. Brent is like…adorable. But he's two years older than me. I don't think my parents will let me go out with him."

"Your parents let you ride in his car all the way to the show and back. What's the difference?"

The girl's face went white.

"You didn't tell them." Emilie lifted an eyebrow as she carried the plates to the table one at a time.

Susan shook her head. "But I didn't lie. They assumed that the other girls from the barn were riding with us. I just didn't correct them." Her head dropped. "I guess I shouldn't have done that."

"No, you shouldn't have," Emilie said. "What if something had happened?"

"Like what?"

"Like a car accident."

"Oh." The girl looked down.

"Talk to your parents, Susan, or I'll have to do it for you."

"Okay."

"And talk to them about Brent, too. He's a nice kid. If it would help, they can ask me about him."

Her blue eyes lit up. "Really? Thanks."

"Don't get too excited. I trust him with horses and he's a good driver. It's not quite the same as trusting someone with a daughter." She set the last place at the table. "Do you have a drink?"

"Yes, thank you. This looks and smells delicious." Susan checked her watch. "I've got to eat fast, though. My dad will be picking me up soon."

"Go ahead. Dig in. And speaking of dads, I'm going to get mine."

Emilie walked to her father's study. In the foyer, a set of suitcases sat in front of the door. Leaving again? The disappointment slowed her pace and made her shoulders droop. "Dad?"

His heavy steps attacked the wooden stairwell. He moved quickly and with purpose. Everything fixed in its place—his hair, shirt, tie, cuffs, belt. All perfect. "Ah, Emilie, you look much better now that you've had a shower."

Thanks. She pointed to the suitcases. "Aren't you staying for dinner? I cooked." *Aren't you even going to ask how I did today?*

He leaned over to kiss her forehead while straightening the Windsor knot, which was already straight. "I'm sorry. I thought I could stay but I can't. I have to get to Florida tonight. I told you I have meetings in Tampa all week."

No, you didn't tell me. She crossed her arms over her chest. "You have your own jet. Can't you fly out later? We need to talk about what the police aren't doing." She didn't bother to mask the irritation in her voice.

"Honey, just let this go. I've got it covered. The police won't give you any more trouble." Her father pulled his overcoat from the hall closet and slipped his long arms into it. "Now, I would love to stay for dinner but the pilot just called. They're having weather in the south. He thinks it'd be better if we took off now. But I promise we'll have dinner when I get back." He lifted his bags and moved to the door.

"Next week?"

For a second, he narrowed his eyes at a blank spot on the wall as if he had access to some invisible calendar hanging there, then he turned back to her. "Two weeks. I'm in Tampa, then in London. I'll be back after Christmas."

After Christmas? Stiffness traveled up her spine. She could feel it chiseling tension into her face.

"I know what you're thinking." Her father stopped in the doorway. "But don't worry, sweetie. I already took care of your present. I'll call you later."

A knot twisted her gut as he walked out, closing the door behind him. Emilie blinked away her tears and lifted her head in the air. She brushed a hand over her sweater, straightening it around her hips and weaved her way back to the kitchen. She wasn't going to cry over her father anymore. He might never change. But she could.

"Dad had to leave." Her voice sounded normal despite the storm of emotions inside.

"Oh no. What about the other steaks?" Susan said.

What about *her* steak? She couldn't eat it. "I can save them."

"Or just give both of them to Derrick," Susan said.

"Maybe." She looked up from her plate to find Susan with a kooky smile spread over her face. "What's *that* look for?"

"He's really cute," Susan said.

Emilie tried to play dumb. "Who? Brent?"

"No. Well…yes, but I meant Derrick. Don't you think he's cute? My mom said he's one of the most handsome men she's ever seen."

Heat crept into Emilie's cheeks. She fanned her face. "Wow. The oven made it really hot in here."

The back doorbell rang. She stepped across the tiled floor, taking a peek through the window. Derrick. She swung open the door. "Come in. We're just getting started. Let me take your coat."

Derrick, all showered and dressed up, filled the room as he stepped in. She relished the clean scent that wafted over her as he walked to the center of the room, his movements stiff and labored. She came behind and reached for his coat, but he transferred the bulky jacket to his other hand.

"I got it, thank you. I—I need to—" His voice sounded different. Strange. "Is your dad here?"

"My dad?" Emilie frowned.

"Yeah." Derrick couldn't meet her gaze, but he could sense the surprise and curiosity in her voice. "I—I need to see him about something."

"Well, you missed him." She walked back to the table, picked up her cloth napkin and sat. "He just left and won't be back for weeks."

Derrick clenched at the bundle in his coat and stared at the floor. A terrible ache throbbed at the center of his forehead. He lifted his free hand and pressed two fingers at its source. Stepping back to the counter behind him, he leaned his hips against it and willed some sense to flow back into his brain. He shouldn't have come over so angry or even considered speaking to Mr. Gill in front of Emilie.

"You're going to join us, right?" Susan said from her place at the large oak table.

Derrick's gaze brushed past the girl, over the empty place across from her, then came to rest on Emilie.

"Of course." He forced a smile.

Emilie pointed to the chair next to Susan. "Take a seat."

Chimes like a church organ echoed through the house.

Susan stood and gave Emilie a quick hug. "That's

my dad. Gotta go. You were awesome today. So glad you beat Jack. I never did like him. Next week, you'l beat that other rider, too. What was her name?"

"Leslie Raney," Emilie answered.

"Whatever." Susan walked to the opening at the opposite side of the kitchen and pointed at Derrick "Don't let her eat alone." She waved a hand through the air, turned and was gone.

Derrick shuffled to the table. His chest tightened at Emilie's cold expression.

"If you don't want to be here," she said, "you don' have to stay."

He locked eyes with her. "Of course I want to be here. I just had something on my mind but I'll take care of it later."

Emilie looked as though she might cry. With a jerky movement, she reached for the untouched plate of food in front of him and walked to the other side of the room. He prayed she wasn't going to throw i away. When she stopped at the microwave, he let ou a deep sigh. He placed his coat and money bundle in a nearby chair.

Not exactly a warm I'm-so-glad-you're-here, bu what was he expecting? She didn't know why he needed to speak with her father. And she certainly didn't know how he felt about her. *The way it needs to stay.* "Now, what can I do to help?" he asked.

"Mine's probably cold, too." She motioned to her plate, which he carried to her. "Help yourself to a drink." She pointed to the fridge.

Derrick reached for a bottle of water, glad he didn't have to worry about envelopes of money stashed beside it.

"Here." She handed him the warm plate. "Go ahead."

He took the steaming plate back to the table where he removed Susan's setting so he could sit next to her. She looked a little surprised as she walked back and took her seat.

"Smells delicious," he said. "Can I bless it?"

"Sure." Her eyes darted around the table avoiding his face.

He reached over and took her hand in his. "Lord, we thank You for this meal that Emilie has prepared. We thank You for this day we've shared together. We thank You for making beautiful horses and for giving Emilie the talent to ride them. We thank You for meeting all our needs. Amen."

When he opened his eyes, Emilie was staring at him. He gave her hand a quick squeeze and then released it, turning quickly to his plate. The savory aromas had tortured his senses long enough. He placed the napkin in his lap and dug in.

Emilie picked at the fish but never took a bite. "You could tell me the message you have for my dad. I could text it to him. Seemed like it was pretty important."

"No. Thanks. I'll talk to him when he gets back." Derrick took a few more bites, hoping she would change the subject.

"Is it about the apartment? Do you need something? I could probably take care of it."

His eyes cut to his jacket in the chair next to him, the wad of money inside its folds—a secret. He knew how hurt she'd be that Camillo had been keeping secrets from her, and he hated that he was doing the same thing. He took a heavy breath, despising Mr. Gill for putting him in this position. He'd thought long and hard over the last week about telling Emilie about the money, but it never felt right. He wanted to give Mr. Gill one more chance to understand that a babysitter was not what Emilie wanted from him. She needed his attention and approval. She needed his love.

He swallowed another bite then took a sip of water. "It's nothing worth talking about tonight."

Her face dropped. "It seems everyone has a secret from me."

Derrick let his head roll back. He couldn't remember when he'd felt like more of a jerk. "I don't want to. But this secret is not mine to tell. Please trust me on this."

A tear slipped down her cheek. "Get out."

"What?" He reached out to touch her face but she pulled back. "Please don't do this, Emilie. I'll tell you what this is about. I will. But not tonight."

"So much for your talk about trust and truth." Her green eyes cut at him.

Derrick grabbed his coat from the chair and turned it over in his hands. Slowly, he removed the envelope from the jacket and placed it on the table. "It's from your father."

Emilie took the packet, looked inside then placed it back on the table. "What did he ask you to do?"

"Nothing really," he said. "Nothing I wouldn't already be doing."

She looked him directly in the eye. "No more secrets, Derrick. What did he ask you to do?"

Derrick dropped his head to his chest. Emilie would hate him for saying it, but he had to tell her. "He wanted me to look after you."

"I see. And this has been going on since you got here." She flinched, fighting not to show the emotions swirling inside her. He could see the pain his words had brought staring back at him in her crystal-like eyes. "I still think you need to leave."

Derrick walked to the door. The food he'd just eaten rising up his throat. "Emilie, despite what you might believe right now, not one thing I have done since coming here has been for your father. Not one. And I will not take his money no matter how many times he offers it."

Emilie listened to Derrick's footsteps fade then she locked the door. Anger had driven her tears away. Humiliation left her so empty she could hardly breathe. She wished she'd been surprised at her father's actions, but she wasn't. She knew what Derrick had said was true. The money on the table proved it. Didn't make it hurt any less. Her father treated her like any other part of his business that didn't need or merit his personal attention. He paid someone else to take care of it. Of her.

He, no doubt, had had the same agreement with Camillo. All that cash in Camillo's account had been from her father. Had Camillo ever been her friend at all? No wonder her father wanted everything covered up and forgotten. All along, he'd been in the middle of this somehow.

Her cell phone buzzed on the countertop. Kind of late for a call. The temptation to ignore it was great. Then again, anything to get her mind off her father would be a welcomed change.

"Emilie Gill," she answered.

"This is Fellman's Security. Your system is reporting fire at the zero-zero-five location. Could you verify? I'm in the process of alerting the local fire department."

Emilie's mouth went dry. Her heart raced. "I don't know. I don't know. I'm not there." She raced to the window. "I can't see that far. Just send them. Send them!"

Emilie grabbed her keys and ran out the back door. She fled down the stone paved path and scrambled into her Jeep.

Her legs shook so violently, she couldn't press the clutch. She turned the key. The engine rebelled with a horrid scraping sound.

Derrick tapped on the passenger window. "Every-thing okay?"

She looked up, hating that she was glad to see him. "The stable is on fire."

FOURTEEN

Derrick slid into the passenger seat without uttering a word. Emilie raced her Jeep down the drive to the barn. The path seemed longer and darker than usual. As the trees parted, an orange glow silhouetted the stables and lit the night sky like a carnival. Smoke swirled overhead.

"Park over there." Derrick pointed to a far corner of the gravel lot. "Leave room for the fire truck."

He leapt from the car before she'd killed the engine. She ran after him, toward the brightness, around the building, down the cold, grassy path. As she turned the final corner, intense heat scorched her skin. Raw, hungry flames licked at the sides of the old barn. Derrick turned her away from the blaze. Spasms of anxiety yanked at her limbs.

"Looks like it's spreading east. Let's go in through the north." He yelled over the crackling blaze. "We'll bring horses out from the west gate."

Emilie followed him in a state of numbness. Panic paralyzed her mind. The responsibility of the animals weighed on her heart like a stone. How could they save fifty horses from this?

They entered through the north side doors. Horses paced and whinnied. Terror reigned over the poor creatures. Smoke heavy as a blanket hung in the air. Emilie followed as Derrick cut through the thickness to the back, closer and closer to the fire. Too close. The flames reached into the new stable, eating away at the fine wood from floor to ceiling like a tunnel of orange and blue.

Emilie stood dazed as Derrick moved in a blur before her, using a blanket to protect himself from the nearby flames. She turned to the stalls. Her pony, Simon, jumped up on two legs to see over the door. Nothing but the whites of his eyes glaring at her. *Oh dear Lord, he was still alive in there.* She unlatched his door. Simon scrambled out and darted away.

Bugs's stall, too, was in flames. She turned to it and froze. Unable to see anything beyond the fire. Two strong hands grabbed her by the shoulders and shook her.

"Open those doors and stand outside." Derrick pointed down the aisle where Simon had run off. "We're gonna put everyone in the west field. Go!"

Emilie didn't move. Everything swirled about her. Heat. Smoke. Fire. The roaring flames filled her ears.

"Go!" Derrick pushed her toward the doors.

Emilie stumbled down the aisle, coughing. She pushed through the west doors. Simon stepped behind her. The panicked clippity-clop of his feet helped her to focus. If she didn't act now, more horses than Bugs would be hurt. Her lungs rejoiced as she moved into the fresh air. She ran the twenty feet to the fence, lifted the chain and pulled the long metal gate perpendicular to the stable. This blocked horses to the left. She stood to the right with her arms spread open.

Simon didn't hesitate but galloped away into the darkness of the large enclosure. His slick coat reflected the blaze behind him as he moved freely, snorting in and out with short, sharp blows.

Seconds later, a brown pony from the stall next to Simon's ran out, then a roan mare and a flea-bitten quarter horse.

"Yah!" Derrick's voice sounded over the blaze. Three more horses stampeded through the doors. Bugs trailed behind, limping on his hindquarters. Emilie gasped, almost unable to believe he could have survived that burning deathtrap he'd been in. She reached into her pocket for her cell and dialed the emergency vet line. Something she would have already done if she'd been thinking clearly. Horses continued to exit. And finally, sirens sounded in the distance.

When the fire trucks arrived, Derrick had rescued over twenty horses. By the time they'd contained the flames, all fifty were out. Exhausted and drained, Derrick and she sat side by side on the tailgate of the emergency vehicle. He breathed from an oxygen tank while she chewed on her nail.

"You okay?" He dropped the oxygen mask.

She nodded, her eyes fixed on a patch of clover below her feet. "Are you?"

"Yes." He lifted the mask back to his face. She could hear him drag the pure oxygen into his lungs.

"Some boarders came to sort out the field. And the emergency vet from Blue Ridge is taking Bugs to her clinic. She had to give him some painkillers. The burns are bad. He may not make it."

"I'm sorry, Emilie."

One of the firemen approached, probably the chief as he tended to bark orders at the others. He stood in front of her with his feet spread wide. "Very fortunate, Miss Gill. The damage was nearly contained to the old structure. Here, follow me. I'll show you."

Emilie swallowed hard. The old back barn might not have been used for horses anymore but it was where she'd spent her childhood. Then, it had been Camillo's home. It had meaning to her. It had harbored life. And death. Now, it had almost completely burnt to the ground.

Derrick walked two steps after the fireman then turned back when Emilie hadn't moved. She shook her head, but he grabbed her hand and pulled her along. She followed, numb and empty. The fireman spoke and pointed to different areas of ruble. She heard bits and pieces. Something about an accelerant.

Something about the point of origin. Finally, he was called away by another worker.

"He didn't say it," Emilie's legs went weak and her body trembled, "but you could tell he thought the fire was deliberate."

"We're going to make this right, Emilie," Derrick whispered.

"I don't understand why someone is doing this," she said. "When you showed me that money, I thought somehow my dad had…" She shook her head. "But he wouldn't have done this."

"No, Emilie. Your father didn't do this." He held his arms open to her.

She fell into his embrace. And for a long time, they just stood there, not moving and not speaking.

"Good luck." Emilie waved to the Daniels family as they drove off. Behind them, a truck and trailer from Winterfield Hills pulled their chestnut thoroughbred to his new home. She didn't blame them for leaving. The fire had spurred several boarders to change barns. Such was the business of boarding— horses always coming and going for some reason or another. Though four leaving in one week had to be a record at Cedar Oaks.

The trailer rolled past the woods and out of sight. A green sedan moved into view. Detective Steele. She'd been dreading the meeting with him. She could only imagine what he'd accuse her of now.

She waited for him at the front door and walked

him to her office. "Can I get you some coffee? A soda?"

"No, thank you." He took the seat across from her desk. "I don't have a lot of time. But I told the fire chief I'd give you his summary."

Emilie's mouth went dry as she sat behind her desk. The detective's grim expression indicated more bad news. Like there was any other kind.

Steele shuffled through some papers in a file he'd brought along. "The fire started where the barns are joined together. Near where we found Mr. Garcia's body. The wind forced the flames back instead of into the new facility. No doubt the fire preferred the old wood over the newly treated."

"What do they think started it?"

"A space heater with faulty wiring. It was melted down pretty badly but they found what was left of it near the last stall of the new facility." He showed her a photo of the model.

"A space heater? We have central heat and air. We don't use space heaters," she said.

"I know." The man stared down at his hands, which fidgeted nervously with the folder of papers. "There were also traces of oil, which served as an accelerant."

"Are you going to tell me that teenagers did this?" she asked.

Steele's mouth parted and he stared up at the ceiling.

"Mr. Steele, I don't know what kind of pressures

you're under to…" she searched for the right words, "to make light of the events occurring here but I am truly hoping that you will ignore them."

His brow furrowed. "Excuse me?"

"You can't possibly think that all these events have been the work of teenagers. Or me trying to cover up a lover's spat."

"As I'm sure you're aware, Miss Gill, the police department is considering your family's peace until something concrete comes to light. Perhaps the serial number on the space heater will tell us something."

"I hope so…I want my name cleared and I want my stable safe. I want my life back and I want Camillo's killer behind bars."

Steele stared hard at her face, his beady eyes at attention. "Yes. Your father made the same demands of our department and at the same time tied our hands."

"He didn't seem to tie your hands when you arrested me." Emilie crossed her arms over her chest.

"You *do* understand that I was merely following the evidence when you were arrested."

"Planted evidence," she said.

"That's your story, Miss Gill. The evidence disappeared from the station before I had a chance to determine that on my own."

"So what are you saying? That I'm still a suspect?" She shook her head. "That's ridiculous. You can't possibly think I would burn down my own barn! I grew up in that barn. That fire burned my stud, the most successful stallion jumper on the east coast! My best chance to make the Olympic team. He'll never jump again." Overwhelmed with emotion, she turned her face to the wall. "He'll never be ridden again."

Steele stood and walked to the door. "I do my job by the book, Miss Gill. I don't need your approval, your criticism or your sob story. But I'll concede the lover's spat theory was the wrong angle. Still, I know there are secrets in this barn. And seeing as you're the owner and operator, I'll still believe we'll find that they're connected to you in one way or another in the end." He turned and walked out.

Derrick had hardly seen Emilie during the week following the fire. She'd carefully avoided him since discovering the truth about her father. Derrick knew she needed some time to sort through her feelings. Waiting in front of the stable, he wondered if she would remember their plan to speak with Hector Emens. Or if, perhaps, now she would prefer to go alone.

"Are you ready?" Emilie walked out looking fabulous in a pair of black dress slacks, a yellow top and a fitted leather jacket.

His mouth dropped open. "Yeah. Uh, let's go."

They walked side by side to the Cedar Oaks truck. Derrick tensed, wondering if he should bring up their last conversation about her father before the fire or just let it go.

"I talked to Blue Ridge Veterinary Hospital," she said. "Bugs is doing great. They're going to keep him there for a month and continue treating his burns. He won't be as pretty as he used to but—"

"That's great news." Without thinking he grabbed her hand and gave it a squeeze.

She stiffened and he quickly released it.

"We should talk," he said.

She looked away. "About what? About my lousy father? About finding out Camillo was paid to be my pal?"

"He may have taken the money, Emilie," Derrick said, "but Camillo was still your friend."

"A friend with a secret," she said. "Something other than the money. Let's just hope Hector Emens can tell us what it was."

"You're not angry with me?"

"I want to be angry at you," she said with a half smile. "I do. You really annoy me sometimes…."

"And other times?"

"You surprise me."

Hector's apartment complex was on the east end of town. Derrick had to drive through it twice before locating Building C. They parked in front of the three-story walk-up. It was old. Gutters hung loose from the roof and some of the white paint peeled from the siding. Emilie looked wary as they made their way to unit fifteen. He put a hand on her lower back and knocked hard at the wood door.

A twenty-something Hispanic man opened the door while slipping a T-shirt over his head. "Señorita Gill."

Emilie nodded. "Call me Emilie, please."

"Come in." The man opened the door wide and shook their hands.

Emilie hesitated but Derrick pressed on her back and she moved forward. The apartment, though small and sparsely furnished, looked clean and homey. They walked into a den where two young children watched cartoons on an old tube-style television. Derrick's stomach rumbled as he inhaled the spicy aromas filling the air. Hector led them to a small round table on the opposite side of the room.

When Emilie didn't speak right away, Hector yelled for the children to go to their room.

"Oh no," Derrick said. *"Que no es necesario."*

Hector smiled, either about the children or perhaps he was relieved that Derrick spoke Spanish. The children jumped up and down then plopped back in front of the television set.

"Por favor, sit." Hector pulled a chair out from the table and sat down. "You'd like a drink?"

"No. *Gracias."* Derrick pulled a chair out for Emilie then took the seat next to her. "Señorita Gill is hoping you could tell her anything you might know about Camillo Garcia. Before his death, he was missing for a full day. He took a job in California but didn't go there. Do you know anything about what happened?"

Hector frowned and scratched his head. "I tell you what I tell police. It all I know. Last two months, Camillo very, very nervous. Tell me he know something and he not know what to do. A few weeks later he said he do the wrong thing and now he must leave."

"Do you know what he did wrong?" Derrick asked.

His eyes fixed on Emilie. "No."

Emilie leaned forward. "You think it had to do with me?"

"*Sí.*" He shrugged. "Or no. Camillo say it about horses, so I think about Señorita. But I never know exactly. Camillo had another problem though I guess you knew that his green card expired."

"Camillo was here illegally?" Emilie gasped. "No. I had no idea. My father took care of that stuff for me."

Hector hesitated. "*Sí.* I believe your father was supposed to help get a new card. But there is some kind of complication."

"What was the complication?" she asked.

"I don't know." Hector stood abruptly as his wife entered the room with two steaming platters of sizzling meats.

Derrick stood, too, and Emilie followed his lead.

"We should be going," Derrick said.

Hector walked them back to the front door. Derrick and Emilie shook his hand and walked back to the truck.

"You think he was telling the truth?" she asked.

"He has no reason to lie to us."

"I wonder what else I didn't know about Camillo Garcia."

Derrick reached a hand to her shoulder for a reassuring touch. His fingers found long, silky tresses resting there, teasing him. And for a second, just a second, he allowed himself to indulge in their softness.

FIFTEEN

"One more time," Emilie shouted.

Derrick whipped his head around and glared at her sitting at the other end of the ring. She laughed at his feigned anger and signaled him over to her place on the fence. She'd seen him jump a few times, but never over fences this large. He seemed easy about it, like he was about everything, even though Duchess was giving him an awful time.

A cold breeze blustered across the hilltop arena and stung her face. Emilie zipped her feather-down jacket up to her chin, rearranged her scarf and pulled at her ski cap. The winds had picked up fast, blowing in a winter storm. Occasional snowflakes scattered down from the sky. Emilie hoped Karin and Max would arrive soon. She didn't want to worry about her sister and brother-in-law stuck in a snowstorm on their way to save her from Christmas without family.

At least the last several days had passed without any incidents occurring at the stable. Perhaps the new security system was keeping the horses safe.

And today was Christmas. She was determined to find some joy in that.

Derrick tried to halt Duchess in front of her, but the chestnut mare danced and sidestepped. He gave up and let her walk in a circle, then punished her by backing her up a few steps. "The deal was one Bible study for one jumper course," he said. "Not five trips over a marathon of fences."

She smiled wide. "Well, it was a terrible deal. You're not having any difficulty at all."

"Au contraire. This mare is hating me, right now."

"Mmm. One more time and let's add an in-and-out." She popped off the railing and headed toward a set of jumps in the center of the ring.

Derrick moaned more pretend annoyance. But she knew that like she, he was having fun.

"You'll love how it feels to jump this high," she added. "Think of it as your Christmas present to me."

"I already have a Christmas present for you. But fine. One more time." He rode off at a quick pace.

She raised a few of the fences to four and five feet, curious what kind of gift Derrick could have bought her for Christmas. When the jumps were ready, she signaled. He began the course without hesitation. But Duchess continued to act strangely. She kicked out and even bucked between some of the jumps. Admittedly, she could sometimes be a difficult mare, but not with Derrick. In fact, Duchess seemed to prefer Derrick over her in the saddle.

Emilie waved her hands in the air. Derrick pulled out of the course and came back to her at the railing.

"What now?"

"Duchess is acting weird," she said. "Let's put her away and get ready for dinner."

"Oh no," he said. "You don't think you've gotten your money's worth, so I'm finishing. One more trip." He rode off and began the course again.

Emilie pressed her lips together as Derrick and Duchess made their way through the course. She counted his strides and held her breath during their hang time. The final vertical and in-and-out, which had been decorated with tinsel for the holidays, made her nervous, especially as Duchess continued to be difficult. Perhaps it was the cold weather making the mare act so. Regardless, Emilie worried and wished the exercise was over.

Another gust of wind swept across the ring. A frigid blast. A sparkling strand of tinsel flapped loose from the final jump.

"Derrick! Stop!" Emilie hopped off the railing and waved her hands in the air again. The wind carried her voice away. Derrick continued through the course.

When the wind came again, the long ribbon of tinsel broke completely free and danced in front of Duchess like a shiny snake. The mare reared then crashed down over the vertical. Derrick clung to her back like the cowboy that he was, but unsettled by the breaking boards, the horse reared again and, blocked by the broken fence, lost her balance and toppled backwards.

Emilie ran toward the tumbling horse and man. Derrick hit the sand first. Then fifteen hundred pounds of equine rolled over him.

Emilie cried out. Panic froze the blood in her veins, but she ran on, heart racing. Frantic with fear that Duchess would stand and trample Derrick all over again, Emilie placed herself between horse and rider. Duchess scrambled to her feet, took one wide-eyed look at Emilie and galloped away.

Emilie turned to Derrick. He wasn't moving. His legs were bent unnaturally under him. His whole figure was pressed into the deep sand. His eyes were closed. Shoulder turned to the side. It pained her to look at him.

"Derrick. Derrick. Talk to me. Open your eyes and talk to me."

His face pinched up tight.

"Okay. Okay. That was movement. Sort of." She released a breath. "Now, talk to me. Come on. Talk."

His lips parted and he took a labored breath.

"Come on, Derrick. Talk. Move your fingers. Move your feet." Her words came out in sharp, short gasps. "Come on. Come on. Show me you can move. Talk to me."

A finger wiggled.

"Yes," she whispered.

He sucked in more air then rolled his upper body to his back. "Where's Duchess?" he mumbled. His eyes flickered open and searched her face.

Duchess? Who cared about Duchess? Emilie danced around in the sand next to him, shaking her head. "Duchess is fine. She's over there." She pointed to the corner of the ring nearest the stable. "Come on, Derrick. Move your legs or I'm calling an ambulance."

"Nah. Calm down, Emilie. Just knocked the wind out of me is all." He coughed and lifted his head. "Where did you say Duchess is? Is she okay? Oh man, we trashed your jump."

"Why aren't you moving your legs?" Emilie knew she sounded frantic. She was. Tears blurred her vision as she bent over and tried to check his pupils. "I think you have a concussion. I'm calling an ambulance." She pulled her cell phone from her coat pocket and flipped it open.

Derrick reached up and grabbed the trim of her coat. "Don't. I'm fine."

She stepped back from his reach, holding the phone to the sky. "Okay then. Get up and I won't call."

"You want me to get up?" He let out a chuckle mixed with more deep coughs. "Ouch." He grimaced and lifted a hand to his head to remove his safety helmet.

"Yes. I want you to get up. I want you to move." She pressed her palms on either side of her face. "This is my fault. This is all my fault."

"Calm down. Not your fault. It was the wind. And I'm okay. I'm just resting."

"You're not okay, Derrick Randall. I'm calling nine-one-one."

She flipped the phone open, but made the mistake of standing too close to him again. This time, he grabbed her knee and pulled hard. She fell to the sand beside him and tried to roll away, but he grabbed her arm, drew her to his chest and pinned her there.

"What are you doing? Let me call."

He grinned, but she saw the pain in his eyes. With her free arm, she reached across his chest for the phone, which had fallen on the other side of him. Derrick's smile widened. He grasped that arm, too, and held them together. The dimple on his left cheek appeared. "No calls."

"This isn't funny, Derrick. You're hurt. Let me call—"

He placed both her wrists in one hand. With the other, he caressed her cheek. His smile faded.

"Come on. Let me call. You're in pain."

"I'm not going to lie to you." He traced his thumb over her bottom lip and then smoothed it back against her cheek. "I'm not feeling too great. But…" His eyes closed and she felt his chest rise and fall with his struggle to breathe. "But I'm going to be fine. Just… just relaxing for a moment."

"You're relaxing?"

Derrick let go of her wrists. "Yep. I'm going to move in just one second."

She didn't believe him. Something was wrong. He was paralyzed or dying and wouldn't let her call for help. She wiggled a hand free and reached over him again for the phone that she'd dropped in the sand. "I'm calling for that ambulance."

Again, he stopped her hand. "No, please."

"Look, you don't want me to call an ambulance, then move your legs right now," she said.

Derrick bit his lip and groaned as his legs moved under him into a more natural position.

Emilie closed her eyes and dropped her head to his shoulder. "Oh, thank God. You can move."

He turned his head to meet her face. A small smile played at his lips. "You thanked God."

"I—I guess I did—"

His hands framed her face. "Emilie…"

Emilie swallowed hard, shaking her head. "I'm sorry, Derrick. I—"

"Shh." He lifted his head and pressed his lips to hers. His touch was warm and gentle.

Emilie closed her eyes and breathed him in. Her hands moved to his shoulders. After a moment, she broke away and lifted up.

"Now for that, I would fall off Duchess a thousand times," he whispered. "Merry Christmas, Emilie."

He smiled, put his hands around her face and pulled her down for another kiss.

"Hey guys! Did you lose something?" A deep male voice called across the ring. "Like a big red horse?"

Emilie hopped to her feet, her lips still tingling from Derrick's touch. Her brother-in-law, Max, and her sister, Karin, stood at the gate with Duchess. "Hey, Karin. Max. Get over here. Derrick is hurt."

She looked back at Derrick. Silent. His eyes closed. How much pain was he really in?

And just when was it that she had fallen in love with him?

SIXTEEN

With a shaky hand, Emilie placed a cup of hot tea next to Derrick, then clasped her hands behind her to hide their shaking.

He tried to smile, but the pain seemed to interfere as he leaned forward for Karin to place some pillows behind his back. Aside from that, he hadn't moved since Max had dumped him into the oversized chair in her den over an hour ago.

"If I'd known I'd get all this attention," he said, looking to her brother-in-law, "I'd have gotten Duchess to roll over me weeks ago. Is this what it's like to be married, Maxie? I could get used to this. Thanks, Karin. Thanks, Emilie."

Max sat on the nearby couch, nibbling a handful of fresh-roasted Virginia peanuts. He gave Karin a not-so-sly wink then narrowed his eyes on his old college buddy. "Marriage? You thinking about getting married, Randall?"

"Well," Derrick said, "once I meet the right Mrs. Randall. Sure."

Marriage? Emilie's eyes went wide. That accident

had rattled Derrick's brain. Did he even know what he was saying?

"I still think we should take you to the hospital," she said. "Please? Max, can't you convince him?"

Max put his palms in the air, clearly finished with trying to talk his friend into seeking medical attention.

"I'm telling you I'm fine." Derrick glared at her. "I don't need a doctor. This is just an old back injury flaring up. A few hours in this chair and a good night's sleep and I'll be good as new."

Emilie rolled her eyes. His mental state worried her, but his stubbornness made her blood boil. Still, she bit her tongue. There was no point in discussing it further. He would not see a doctor. He'd made that perfectly clear. Even though he had to know as well as she that if her brother-in-law hadn't shown up and helped him, he'd still be laid out flat on his back in the middle of the riding ring. Stubborn man.

Frustrated, she returned to the kitchen where her pork roast and winter squash casserole waited for Christmas dinner. Since Derrick couldn't sit at the dining room table, she prepared four trays to carry to the den.

"Can I help?" Karin asked from the doorway.

"Sure. Just grab these." She pointed to the trays.

"Smells so good. You cook just like Mom," Karin said. She came next to Emilie and put an arm around her shoulders.

Tears built in Emilie's eyes. "Don't. You're going to make me cry."

"I know. I miss her, too." Karin gave Emilie a squeeze. "Mom wouldn't have put up with Dad being away for the holidays."

"No. She wouldn't have," Emilie agreed.

"I think that's why he's not here, don't you?" Karin said.

"What do you mean?" Emilie stepped away to prepare the dinner plates.

Karin frowned, following her with the napkins and silver. "He misses her. He can't deal with it."

"So, he'd rather be in a hotel three thousand miles away? I don't understand that."

Karin pushed her short auburn hair behind her ears. "It's called escapism."

"Rosa told me he's been drinking again."

Karin frowned and stepped back. "I was afraid of that. I'll talk to him. It's been two years since Mom died. He needs to stop hiding away in his work and pick up the pieces."

"He was trying to pay Derrick off to take care of me. Can you believe that?"

"So typical of him," her sister said. "Trying to fix everything in the wrong way. But don't be angry. I'm sure he meant well."

"I'm not so sure," Emilie said. "He had secrets with Camillo. Sometimes I wonder if—"

"Don't go there, Emilie," Karin said. "You're

hurt. You don't mean what you're saying. Dad could never…"

Emilie clenched her teeth. Her faith in her father had diminished to something nearly nonexistent and her sister would never understand. "Do you think Derrick will be okay?"

"Max seems to think so…." A gentle smile lightened Karin's expression. "You two seem to have gotten close."

"Good grief, Karin. You say that every time I spend more than five minutes with a man." Emilie turned to hide the blush she knew was coming to her cheeks.

Karin folded her arms across her chest. "And you've spent more than five minutes with what… about three men?"

"Are you counting?" Emilie glared at her playfully. "Come on. Let's eat. Grab those." She pointed to two of the trays she'd prepared and followed her sister into the den with the others.

Max prayed over the meal. Emilie noticed the glowing look on Max, Karin and Derrick's faces as Max talked of Jesus' birth and death. As she looked over their faces she longed for the peace she saw inside them. Why couldn't it belong to her?

Max ended by praying for Derrick's recovery.

"Amen to that," Derrick said as he dug into the dinner. "Delicious," he added, smiling at her.

At least his appetite hasn't been affected, Emilie thought.

"It is normal for a show horse to get so spooked at a fence?" Karin asked.

"Yes," Derrick said.

"No," Emilie said over him. Derrick didn't want her to feel badly about the injury. But he knew the mare should not have behaved the way she did. "Duchess was acting strangely."

"She just didn't like the way I jump. She probably didn't like the extra hundred pounds on her back. She is used to you," he said.

Emilie made a doubting face.

Karin frowned. "I saw the damage to the barn. That fire must have been something."

"It was horrible," Emilie said. "Bugs will never compete again. Camillo's apartment and most of the old barn were destroyed. But Steele has some hope that the space heater will lead to something. He's sent it to a forensic specialist in Washington."

After dinner, Max and Karin collected the empty plates and declared it their duty to wash the dishes. Awkwardness filled the room. Suddenly, Emilie could think of nothing but that Derrick had kissed her the last time they'd been alone. She fumbled under the tree and located his present.

"Thanks." He took the small box from her. "Should I wait for the others?"

She shook her head. "No, go ahead."

Derrick undid the fancy bow she'd spent fifteen minutes tying to perfection and slid the box open.

He drew out the ticket she'd placed inside and read it. The permanent grin dropped from his face.

She moved to his side. "Are you in pain again?"

"Shock. Emilie. I'm in shock. This is too much. I can't possibly accept this." He held up the plane ticket to San Salvador where his parents lived. "It's too much," he continued.

Disappointed with his response, she shook her head. "You don't want to visit your family?"

"You know I do." He smiled again and touched her hand. "It's just…I know how much it costs to fly to San Salvador. I can't believe you did this. Thank you."

"So you like it?"

"I love it."

The grateful expression on his face filled her with satisfaction. "You have a year to use it, which is good. I don't think you'll be jetting off any time soon."

"No." He looked down at his legs.

She kneeled beside his chair. "Are you going to be okay, Derrick? Tell me the truth."

He stared into the orange flames of the gas fire nearby. "It's a pinched nerve. If it doesn't get better in a day or two, I'll let you take me to a doctor."

A pinched nerve. Those were operable, right? She let out a sigh of relief. "Promise?"

"Promise." He let go of her hand and pointed to a large box on a table near the Christmas tree. "That's for you. I'm afraid it's not much compared to this ticket."

Emilie moved over to the gift. "You shouldn't have gotten me anything."

Derrick looked somber while she opened the box. Inside was a crunched piece of metal. She pulled it out and stared. "Is it a precious metal I'm unfamiliar with?"

He chuckled. "Nope. It's what's left of our crash. Remember?"

"The trailer? How could I forget?"

Derrick smiled warmly again. "Well, the metal-works guy at the shop wouldn't work on it. So, I fixed it myself."

"Are you kidding?"

"No. I've been working on it at night. It looks pretty good. I replaced the divider and put in better flooring. The brakes have been repaired and it's been inspected. It's all ready to go."

"Wow. Thank you," she said, as a few tears threatened to fill her eyes. No one had ever given her a gift they'd worked on with their own hands—a gift of time and consideration beyond the seconds it took to order the designer earrings her father had left her or the gift certificate that Max and Karin had given. She felt warm all over as she thought about the hard hours he must have put in.

"You have to promise not to pull it in the snow," he teased.

"No worries." She chuckled and walked to the

window. "I'm not listening to the weather reports ever again. Just like today. All this snow we were supposed to get and we have flurries. And that day, they said the storm would blow over and we had a small blizzard."

"Hey, Emilie, I uh…" His voice dropped off.

She turned around. His face looked pale and drawn. "What is it?"

"Well, right after the accident with Duchess I…" He paused again. "I'm afraid I acted inappropriately. I hope I didn't offend you."

Offend her? With the best kiss of her life? She hoped he couldn't read the confusion and disappointment she felt at his words. Had it been so bad for him? Was he not attracted to her the way she was to him? She understood that she was his boss and it was inappropriate, still she hated hearing him say it. In fact, she would have preferred he not mention it at all.

"Hey, I'm the one who said you were acting crazy." She backed to the doorway. "Excuse me. I'm going to see if they need any help putting things away in the kitchen."

She turned and walked out.

Should he not have apologized? It had seemed like the right thing to do, even though what he really *wanted* was to kiss her again. Derrick shook his head in self-disgust. What *he* wanted was not the point.

There could be no future between them.

That was the point.

Even if Emilie gave her heart to the Lord—something he prayed for daily—they were from different worlds. He'd never be able to give her the things she was used to. He prayed the kiss hadn't ruined their friendship.

Derrick closed his eyes. The pain in his head and back had him on the verge of insanity. It had been all he could do to make it to this chair and that had been with a lot of help. He thanked God that Max and Karin had shown up when they did, because otherwise, Emilie would have called an ambulance. Then he'd have medical care he couldn't pay for.

The accident had been a brush with death. A Christmas day wake-up call. A slap in the face. *Okay God. I get it. I need to get moving with my life. Find my purpose. Time to grow up.* It was just a shame that this realization had come after his adrenaline-fueled kiss and not before. Not that he wanted to erase that kiss—far from it—but he hated that it had led to Emilie fleeing the room with that hurt look in her eyes.

Gritting his teeth through the searing pain, Derrick placed his feet on the floor.

"Don't get up yet," Karin said. She and Max walked into the room with coffee and pecan pie. "You still look pale."

"With all this tea I've been drinking, I'm going to have to get up sooner than later."

"After dessert. Max can help you." Karin handed

him a slice of pie and placed his coffee on the table beside him.

"Thank you." He looked toward the kitchen. No sign of Emilie. His gut clenched.

"She went to feed the horses and look at the trailer you fixed up for her." Max lifted an eyebrow. "We're kind of glad because we hoped you would tell us what's really going on."

"Going on?" Derrick repeated.

"Yes, at the stable. Tell us what Emilie is leaving out," Karin said.

Derrick's frown deepened. "I don't know but I think Camillo Garcia was in something over his head."

Karin's expression filled with worry. "Like what? Something illegal?"

"No idea." Derrick shook his head, staring at the slice of pie. "But whatever it was, I think it had something to do with Emilie, the horses or," he looked at Karin, "your father."

Max let out a whistle.

Now, her face turned white. "Why do you say that?"

"Camillo had secrets and one of them was that he'd lost his green card. Word is that Mr. Gill was holding it over him. But I don't know." Derrick continued, "That can't be all of it. He had a girlfriend, too. If we could figure out who she was maybe we could get some answers."

"Girlfriend?" Max lifted an eyebrow. "Doesn't

Emilie know who Camillo was dating? They were so close."

Derrick shook his head. "She doesn't, which makes me think it's someone at the stable. Maybe even someone married. Why else keep it such a secret?"

"Well, you can scratch Preston off your list of bad guys," Max said. "Mr. Gill makes some strange choices about Emilie but I can't believe he'd ever do anything to hurt her or her horses."

"He wouldn't," Karin said. "And speaking of hurting Emilie—"

"Yes, we asked Emilie already, but she played dumb," Max interrupted.

Derrick shrugged his shoulders. "I guess I'm feeling dumb, too. You lost me." He took a bite of pie. "Oh, man. Did Emilie make this?" He shoved another bite of the nutty, buttery concoction into his mouth.

Karin and Max eyed each other then focused on him again.

"We saw you kissing," Max said.

"Oh. Well, I guess that does deserve an explanation." Derrick sighed. "It was…a moment of weakness and temporary insanity on my part. I apologized to her. I'm afraid that's all there is to it."

Max snickered, but Karin's freckled cheeks flushed with emotion. She pushed her dessert aside.

"Derrick, my little sister is…" Her eyes searched through the room, then came back to his face. Their intensity reminded him of Emilie's hot looks when she argued with him. "She's not experienced with men. If you don't have feelings for her... You can't just... I don't want you to break her heart."

"Whoa. I didn't say I didn't have feelings for her." Derrick stared back at the couple. What about *his* heart?

Karin shook her head. "I'm just saying don't start something you can't finish."

His jaw clenched. *You're not good enough, Randall.* That was really what Karin meant. Her words sucked the air out of the room.

Derrick placed his plate on the table next to his coffee and pressed his hands to the arms of the chair. He had to move. Get air. Escape Max and Karin's unwarranted scrutiny. He pushed up, grunting at the sharp pain attacking his lower back.

Max hurried to help. Neither man spoke as they slowly made their way out of the Gills' house and up to his apartment.

"You're moving better," Max said, as he eased Derrick onto his sofa.

"You think?" Derrick attempted a laugh.

"A little. Can you make it the rest of the night without help?" his friend asked.

"Doubt it. You and Karin staying?"

"Yeah, for a few days."

Derrick leaned his head back into the cushions and let out a deep sigh. "Good. Can I call you later?"

"Of course." Max gave a single nod and stared

out the large picture window that looked over the gardens. "Can I sit down for a sec?"

"Sure." Derrick gestured halfheartedly to a nearby chair. He didn't want a lecture about Emilie. On the other hand, it comforted him that someone looked out for her best interests. Her father certainly didn't.

Max sat on the edge of a slip covered chair next to the couch. He placed his elbows on his knees and his chin on his fists. "I just want to say I'm sorry. We were too blunt about Emilie. Karin worries about her. She didn't mean it like it sounded. We know your integrity. It's not really our business. If you guys like each other, then—"

"No. It's not like that. And Karin's right to care about her sister. But she doesn't need to worry. Not about me, anyway. I would never hurt Emilie. I can promise you that. Anyway, Emilie's a lot tougher than you think. You need to come to a show. She's amazing to watch and I know it would mean a lot to her to have you there."

"That'd be good. I'll talk to Karin." Max stood. "I can tell you're tired. I'll get out of here and check on you in a bit."

"Thanks. And tell Karin there's nothing to worry about. That kiss only happened because the accident rattled my bones and my brains. It won't happen again. Any normal day, I know I don't have anything to offer a woman like Emilie."

Max nodded, scratched his head and chuckled on his way to the door.

"Is that funny?" Derrick asked.

His friend turned back and smirked. "Yes. It's pretty funny. It's exactly what I used to say to myself when I first met Karin."

SEVENTEEN

The next two weeks passed slowly for Emilie. Besides workouts with Mr. Winslow, the stable was quiet—no shows over the holidays, boarders on vacation, her father still in Europe. Even Derrick had taken a few days to visit his uncle. She missed him. She missed his smile and his deep laughter, of which she'd heard little since the accident. And the kiss.

At six o'clock, as she always did, Emilie closed up the stable, turned on the new alarms and headed home, expecting to spend another night alone. But parked in back of the house, she found Derrick's car and her father's. Not having expected either of them, the pleasant surprise caused her to smile. Across the garden, she saw the indoor pool facility illuminated. She followed the garden path to the long brick building. Peeking through the steamy windows, she watched Derrick's long, lean body cut through the water. She and Derrick had hardly spoken since the accident. Stupid kiss. When would they get past it? Could they get past it?

Her father's sudden exit from the pool house drew her eyes up. "Daddy, welcome back." At first she smiled, but then unable to push away the thought of the money Derrick had shown her, she filled with anger.

"Hi, sweetheart." He gave her a quick but tight hug.

"When did you get home?" she asked.

"A couple of hours ago." He tightened the towel that covered his wet head.

"Great. Maybe we could have dinner? I'd like to ask you about something."

"Not tonight. I have a videoconference." He gave her a kiss on the forehead then moved toward the house.

She stared after him, the sting of his negligence biting deeper than ever.

Her father turned back at the arbor near the patio. "Oh, I almost forgot to tell you. This Sunday, I'm coming to your show. I just spoke with Derrick about it. I believe your sister and Max will be there, too."

Her eyes widened. "Great. I'll get you into Winslow's skybox."

Stunned, she entered the pool house and sat in a corner, waiting for Derrick to finish his workout. Her father at a horse show? He hadn't been to one since her mother had died. If he did come, it would mean…well, it would mean something.

Derrick continued to swim lap after lap. Emilie lost her thoughts in the slow, steady rhythm of his strokes until his head finally lifted from the water. He leaned against the side of the pool and took some heavy breaths.

"Hi," she said.

"Emilie. I…" He pulled off his goggles and

lifted himself from the pool without so much as a grimace.

She couldn't help staring at the beautiful cuts of muscle in his chest and abdomen, while her mind reeled with heavy emotions, a mix of tenderness and sadness and even fear. She wanted to move closer, but couldn't seem to budge from her spot in the corner. Why had a silly kiss changed so much? She didn't understand, but as hard as she tried, she couldn't look at Derrick Randall the same way.

"I didn't see you come in," he said. "I thought you were at Peter's."

"I was. I thought you were visiting your uncle in Tennessee." She smiled.

He stopped rubbing his head with the towel and returned her smile. "I didn't want to test my riding skills on your million-dollar horses so I rode at my uncle's. You know, some backyard ponies. Went to a chiropractor, too. I'm all fixed up. He said to swim some and get another adjustment in a few weeks."

"That's great news. I was worried." Emilie fidgeted with her hands, unable to relax. She wanted to hug Derrick, not stand twenty yards from him. "And I was at Mr. Winslow's for a few days. I took the trailer. It did well. Thanks for fixing it." *I missed you*.

"Good." He nodded and dressed in some sweats that had seen better days.

"Duchess is fine," she continued. "Cindy looked her over and couldn't find a thing wrong with her."

"Just no more tinsel." He gripped the towel hanging around his neck.

"Right. No more tinsel. I'm sorry about making you ride that course."

The muscles in his cheek flexed. "It wasn't your fault, Emilie. If anyone should say they're sorry, it should be—"

"No!" She held up her hands. *Don't talk about the kiss.* "I want to be friends again. Please, can we get past that?"

His gray eyes softened. "I'd like that. Do you have plans for dinner?"

"No."

"Maybe we could order a pizza?" he offered.

"How about I make a pizza?" She smiled.

"Even better."

"Then meet me in the kitchen in fifteen minutes?"

He nodded. She turned and left the pool house.

Fifteen minutes. She hoped it was enough time to settle her emotions and forget about that perfectly carved abdomen.

"I can't believe my dad and Max and Karin are coming this Sunday to the show." Emilie beamed, her green eyes wide and twinkling.

Derrick smiled and watched her bite into the deep-dish pizza piled high with every imaginable topping. He took a deep breath and tried to calm himself. Why couldn't he relax? He picked up his soda and took a long drink.

"I also talked to Mr. Adams today about the case," Emilie continued.

"Really?" Derrick nodded. "What did he say?"

"He and my father have word that the police have come up with something about that space heater. A connection to someone."

"So they might be close to making an arrest?"

She nodded. "It's possible. Wouldn't that be great?"

"It would be great to know that you're safe, Emilie."

Her cheeks reddened.

"Are you going to rebuild?" he asked, wishing he hadn't made her uncomfortable.

"No." She sighed. "I'm going to repair Bugs's stall. And add a storage room. But I'm not going to rebuild the old barn. It's gone." She looked him in the eyes. "It wouldn't be the same."

No, nothing will be the same. Derrick studied her expression. She couldn't have made that decision with ease. But she spoke in a calm tone, showing little emotion. He wished his own heart felt as settled.

But inside, he struggled. He struggled with his affection for her, her lack of faith and God's calling for his life. The accident had given him focus. He knew what and where God had called him. Once things settled at the stable… Once he knew Emilie and her horses were safe, he'd head back to school. And leave Emilie.

EIGHTEEN

"I am not going to withdraw Marco from competition just because you had a little scare." Emilie turned on her heels and stomped up the ramp of the trailer.

"A little scare?" Derrick's voice cracked with emotion. "You didn't see it. He threw me sky-high. It was a miracle I landed on my hands and knees."

Her back to him, she stopped and closed her eyes. *Yes. Thank goodness you didn't get hurt again.* She pressed her lips together and turned back to face him. "Don't yell in the trailer. You'll upset the horses."

Derrick rolled his eyes and trudged up the ramp after her. "Fine. I won't yell. But don't ride that horse. Something is wrong with him. He's unpredictable. You need to have the vet check him out. But please don't ride him today."

"I appreciate your concern. But don't you think you're just nervous after your accident with Duchess? Marco will be okay. Something in the practice ring probably spooked him."

"No. Nothing spooked him." Derrick's voice

teetered on the edge of hysteria. "I'm telling you, something is wrong with him. I don't know what. If I didn't know better, I'd say it was the same thing that was wrong with Duchess on Christmas Day. But that's not the point right now. The point is he's not safe. You can't ride him until he has a thorough exam."

"Can't?" she repeated with wide eyes. Was he ordering her? Her cheeks filled with heat. She walked to the corner of the trailer where Marco stood in his ties, nibbling on a net of hay. He looked half-asleep.

"I just don't want you to get hurt. It's not worth the risk," he whispered behind her.

"Marco has made more jump-offs this season than either Chelsea or Duchess. What I can't risk is taking him out. Anyway, look at him. He looks fine."

"He looked fine before he went berserk," Derrick mumbled. "You'll see what I mean as soon as you get him under saddle. Something is wrong." He stepped close to her again, taking hold of her by the elbow. "I don't know much in this world, Emilie, but I know horses. I'm begging you. Don't ride that horse today." The pleading look in his eyes wrenched her heart.

"Miss Gill," Mr. Winslow appeared at the bottom of the ramp. "I hate to intrude on a private moment but we must hurry. It's time to study the course. I've been waiting for five minutes."

She pulled away from Derrick. "This is hardly a private moment. Derrick is being ridiculous."

"Ridiculous?" The trainer took a couple of steps up the ramp. His eyes darted from Derrick to her and then back to Derrick again.

"Something's wrong. Marco is up. She needs to withdraw him from the show," Derrick said.

Mr. Winslow frowned. "Well, I can see her hesitation. The Olympic Selection Committee will notice if he's out. Today's show is critical. It's on Sports Network."

Derrick threw his hands in the air. "I know the stakes. I wouldn't say this if I didn't think Emilie would be in danger. You two are talking about TV and the Olympics. I'm talking about her life! I know this is your decision, Emilie. Just…make the right one."

Her resolve weakened at the look of desperation in his face. She turned to Mr. Winslow.

"Miss Gill, there is no one on Earth whose opinion on horses I value above my own, with the exception of this young man. It is your decision but I urge you to consider his advice."

Emilie tried to think over her safety, but that had never been a concern. Neither were her thoughts on the Olympics or Sports Network. It was her father she thought of, up in the skybox waiting for her to ride. After all this time, he'd come to watch her. He expected her on three horses. And that meant she would ride three horses.

She turned back to Derrick, hardly able to endure

the pitiful look in his eyes. "I'm sorry. I need to ride, Derrick. Warm up Chelsea. She's first out."

He stared at her like she'd stabbed him in the heart with a ten-inch blade.

"Please understand. This is a big day for me. It's not just about winning. I know you had a little fall. But that doesn't mean I will."

Without a word, Derrick walked to Chelsea. His unspoken anger and disappointment shouted volumes in the small space. But Emilie had to shake it off. Her whole family would be watching, not to mention the Olympic Selection Committee. She would ride Marco. She had to. On weak legs, she scrambled down the ramp to Mr. Winslow and together they headed to the main arena.

Within a minute, Derrick caught them. "There's still time for you to change your mind. I pray you will." Before she could respond, he strode away with Chelsea at his heels.

"He doesn't understand," she said to Mr. Winslow.

The trainer didn't respond.

After studying the course, Emilie walked up to Winslow's skybox and knocked on the door.

Max smiled as he let her in. "I can't believe you're going to jump higher than those amateurs. I don't think I can watch."

"Well, that would be a waste of a perfectly good skybox," she said with a wink. It felt good to be with her family, have them there, supporting her, cheering her on. If only Derrick could understand why she wasn't heeding his advice, the day would be perfect.

Max and Karin gave her bear hugs. Her father walked over and kissed her on the forehead. As he pulled away, she saw tears glistening in the corners of his eyes.

"I haven't seen you in your riding…" He pressed his lips together. "You look so much like your mother. Do well today."

Karin was right. Her father did the wrong things, but he did them for the right reasons. Moved by the tears and the weakness in his voice, Emilie flung her arms around her father's neck. "I will, Daddy." *For you, I will.*

The second Emilie mounted Marco, she wished she had listened to Derrick. The horse was loose, uncollected, trembling underneath her. Something was definitely wrong. Was this what Duchess had felt like the day of his accident? No wonder he'd been so suspicious. She now wondered how he'd made it through a course at all.

As she trotted Marco into the ring, he paddled his forelegs and pressed hard to the right. He flung his head up and down. When the buzzer sounded for her to begin, he kicked out. It was going to be a fight. A ninety-second battle of wild equine versus tiny rider.

And all on national television.

Emilie expelled the negative thoughts from her head with a deep sigh and focused on the course. *Find a rhythm,* she coached herself.

There was no rhythm. Marco added steps before every fence, he crow hopped on some of the landings and he kicked out on the flat. Somehow they cleared the first half of the course and for a moment, Emilie had a small hope they might finish.

Then, as Derrick had put it, Marco went berserk. His entire body altered from trembling awkwardness to what felt like surges of wild rage. For the first time ever, Emilie feared for her life on the back of a horse.

Her pulse raced and thumped hard against her chest, she tried to reason through her options. What to do? Jumping off the horse at this pace was not an option. Already aimed at the next fence, Emilie pushed Marco with her left leg, signaling him to run out to the right. Two refusals and they'd be disqualified. She could leave the ring. People would think they'd had a bad day. It happened sometimes. No big deal. But Marco did not run out. He plowed through the jump and took three rails with him.

The crowd gasped.

At the next fence, she pushed him again to the right. Marco ran out, but not to the right. He went left. Emilie clung to him with her legs but the sudden change in direction popped her neck, sending sharp pains through her spine.

Finally, Marco slowed, but not without flinging

his head around in defiance. Emilie signaled the officials that she was withdrawing and headed out of the ring as fast as she could.

Derrick stood in the passageway between the arena and outdoor trailer parking. He had Duchess in hand, whom she was to ride next. Emilie dismounted and nearly collapsed to the ground.

Derrick grabbed the reins from her and stood between the two horses. "I'd like to sedate him with Shen Calmer for the ride home."

Emilie nodded her consent. Shame filled her head. She couldn't lift her eyes to Derrick.

He placed Duchess's reins in her hands and leaned down to whisper in her ear. "Emilie, you did what you had to do. Now go do what you know how to do." He turned and strode away, keeping a tight hand on Marco.

I'm sorry. Deep emotions trapped her voice. Tears blurred her vision. She'd have to tell Derrick later when she could find the words. And maybe she wouldn't just say she was sorry. Maybe she would tell him how she really felt. Maybe she would tell him that she loved him.

Derrick did not want to meet with Mr. Gill. But he didn't see how he could refuse the man's invitation to the skybox without being rude. He knocked at the door, hoping to breeze in and out then get back to work as fast as possible. He'd never been more ready for a day of work to end in his entire life.

Mr. Gill opened the door and motioned for him to enter. Derrick glanced around the luxury box. Karin, Max and Peter were all absent. His chest tightened and he prayed for the Lord to help him through this uncomfortable moment.

"A drink?" Mr. Gill held up a half-filled cocktail glass.

"No. Thank you, sir."

Emilie's father turned and gazed out of the large glass windows overlooking the arena. Below, a tractor dragged wires over the sand and a small crew prepared new fences for the Grand Prix jump-off.

"So, now Emilie rides that brown horse again?" Mr. Gill asked.

"Yes sir, Chelsea. And the thoroughbred, Duchess." Derrick looked over the new course. It appeared to be a good setup for Emilie. "She and three other riders made the jump-off. From the looks of this course, it will be all about the time now. Your daughter should win on Chelsea. She's fast. Duchess will be third. Fourth, if she's feeling lazy."

Mr. Gill downed the remainder of his drink. "You're a bright man, Mr. Randall. You must know that I didn't ask you up for a chat about the jump-off. I called you here because I did not like what I saw today. I thought you and I had an understanding."

"No, sir. I don't believe that we did."

The man spun around, slamming his cocktail glass on the counter. "This isn't about money. This is about my daughter's safety. You took this job. You protect my daughter. That's the deal."

Derrick swallowed hard. "Protect her? You want her protected? Then let the police do their job. You tie their hands thinking a low profile is best when in truth you're leaving the stable and Emilie in danger."

"I know what I'm doing," Mr. Gill growled. "Don't blame what happened today on me. You let her ride a crazed horse. I saw it with my own eyes."

Derrick kept his eyes steady, his head high. "Believe what you will. I have done everything in my power to protect your daughter."

"I ought to fire you right here and now." Mr. Gill stood inches from his face. His breath smelled of liquor. His face pinched with anger. "I trusted you with one of my most precious, most valued, most cherished possessions. You let her go out there and practically get herself killed. You and Winslow should be hanged."

"Your most valued possession?" Rage pulsed through Derrick's veins. He couldn't believe what he was hearing. He wanted to punch the lights out of the man. Instead, he closed his eyes and asked God to direct his words. A great calm flowed over Derrick. He took a deep breath and relaxed his hands and his voice. "Emilie is not a possession. She's a human being with feelings and brains and guts I can't even begin to comprehend. You want to know why your daughter rode that horse today? Why she knocks herself out training? And sets her goals so high? For you. She does it all for you. She craves your love, your attention, your affection. And you give her nothing. You want to blame someone for the risk she took today, blame yourself, because I had nothing to do with it."

"How dare you talk to me like that about my own daughter!"

"You don't frighten me, Mr. Gill. And you don't need to fire me. As soon as I know the threat at the stable is resolved, I'll be leaving." Derrick walked to the door.

"What threat at the stable?"

Derrick stopped and looked back. "The murder, the fire, the cut brake line... Someone is out to destroy the things your daughter cares about."

"It was kids. Vandals." Mr. Gill waved a dismissive arm through the air.

"I don't believe that and I know you don't either."

"You told her, didn't you? About the money." Worry and grief covered the older man's face.

Derrick placed his hand on the door. "Your daughter can't rest until she finds out what happened to Garcia. She deserves the truth. The longer you keep the police from doing their job, just to keep your name out of the paper, the longer you make her unhappy and keep her under threat."

"You need to learn your place, son."

"I know mine, sir. Do you know yours?" Derrick

met Mr. Gill's hard green gaze and saw something in them he'd never seen before. A glimmer, a hint of respect.

NINETEEN

"So, how's this new security system working out?" James Joyner eyed the camera that had been mounted over the west entrance. He pulled Babbit's back leg between his knees and began to file.

"Oh. So far, it's great." Derrick held Babbit's lead rope with a loose hand, half listening to James' prattle. His mind was still stuck on Marco. "There's a camera over each entrance and at night a laser motion detector that cuts through the aisles. The tack rooms and offices have full room motion detection."

"Well, seems to have quieted things down, huh?" James dropped the horse's leg and wiped the sweat from his forehead.

"I don't know. I don't think I'll sleep well until I know who was behind all of it."

James nodded slowly and moved to Babbit's other side. "So, how are things with Mr. Gill?"

Derrick frowned.

James looked back at him when he didn't answer. "I heard he was pretty upset with you about what happened with Marco at the show yesterday."

That was some fast-traveling gossip, even by barn standards. Derrick cleared his throat. "I wasn't too happy about it, either. There is no sensible reason for Marco to have behaved that way. I called Dr. Saunders. In fact, she'll be here any minute. I hope she'll be able to run some tests."

"Oh yeah, Dr. Saunders will take care of it," James said. "You can be sure of that. She's the best."

Derrick had his doubts about that. When Duchess had rolled over him on Christmas Day, Emilie had asked Cindy to run tests on the mare. She had done so with great reluctance and then taken offense when he'd asked to read the lab results himself. The tests had been clean but for some reason Derrick felt he couldn't trust that. Horses, like people, didn't go nuts for no reason.

"James Joyner?"

Derrick and James turned at the unfamiliar voice. Detective Steele and another police officer stood in the aisle. Emilie was behind them, a sick expression in her eyes.

James dropped Babbit's leg and stepped forward. "I'm James Joyner."

The officer moved in and pulled out his cuffs. "James Joyner, you are under arrest for arson in the case of fire at Cedar Oaks Stables. For breaking and entering. For animal cruelty…"

Derrick backed away from the scene after securing Babbit in the ties, then he turned to Emilie. "What happened?"

"They linked the sale of the space heater to a credit card in the farrier's name and got a warrant for his home. Inside they found a set of keys to my stable and containers of amphetamines and Ace."

Derrick shook his head. "But James? Why? What could Joyner have to gain by hurting your horses?"

"I don't know." Emilie shook her head. "But Ace is what Camillo was given before he was killed."

"Yes, Emilie, but lots of farriers use Ace. And this is James. It makes no sense."

"Hey, you're the one who said it was someone at the stable." She stepped away. "Can you handle things here for a bit? My father wants me to come up to the house and talk."

"Sure," Derrick said as she walked off. *I need to talk to you, too.*

Emilie turned away, but Derrick watched dumbfounded as the police tucked James inside the back of the squad car. Derrick studied the farrier's face, expecting anger, rage, fury. Instead, he saw confusion and sorrow.

"I heard James Joyner was arrested for the fire," Cindy said as she got to work on the big black gelding.

Marco groaned a few times while she poked and prodded him, but did nothing more. His lids hung half-closed and he held his neck low like he might take a nap. A complete one-eighty in behavior in such a short period of time usually pointed to one thing—drugs.

He scratched his head and turned to Cindy. "Yes. The police just towed his truck away."

"So, what happened?"

"Apparently, James owned the heater that started the fire."

Her eyes went wide. "Wow. That's...hard to believe."

"I agree. I can't make any sense of it...kind of like this horse. I can't make any sense of his behavior yesterday." Derrick shook his head, hoping she wouldn't ask more questions about the arrest. He wanted her focused on the gelding.

Cindy looked irked at the change in subject. "Too bad I didn't see it for myself. That might have helped," she said, "because so far, I detect nothing wrong with him. He looks perfectly fine."

She walked to her bag and pulled out an equine thermometer. "You know, Derrick, we never did cash in that rain check."

"Excuse me?" He recalled vaguely her once inviting him to dinner. He hadn't wanted to go then. He didn't want to go now.

Cindy lifted an eyebrow. "Dinner. You. Me. Remember?"

"Right." Derrick plastered a smile on his face.

"How about tonight?" She locked eyes with him as she continued pressing her fingers hard into different sections of Marco's abdomen, feeling for abnormalities.

"Actually, I—uh…" He scrambled for a viable excuse to say no.

"I know a great Italian place," she continued.

Bet they don't make veal piccata as good as Emilie's. Derrick kept the fake smile on his face. "I'll check my schedule."

"Great." She continued the examinations along his barrel, checked his eyes, his colon. Finally, she stopped, peeled the long glove from her arm, disposed of it in a nearby trash bin and shook her head. "I don't feel anything abnormal. I don't see anything. I say we take some X-rays and draw blood. I'll bring the film in from my truck. You should go check your calendar."

"Right." He hitched Marco to the wash stall but he didn't go back to his office to check his schedule. He knew he had no plans. So, what could he say? Bowling? Late riding lesson?

Cindy returned with her equipment. Derrick busied himself positioning the film under Marco's forelegs wondering why they were taking X-rays. There was nothing wrong with his legs. Why wasn't she asking more questions about his behavior at the show? Why didn't she ask if he'd been given any medications for traveling or for injuries? And there were several other tests that she might run. Cindy hadn't mentioned any of them.

"So, how long have you performed the herbal joint

therapy on Marco?" he asked. "Maybe Marco had a bad reaction to the last injection?"

"Not possible." Cindy got her camera and squatted in front of the horse's legs. "He's been having those injections for over a year. And he's jumped better and better since he started. I think he and Emilie are shoo-ins for the Olympic team, don't you?"

Derrick felt his brows come together. Joint therapy of any kind should maintain a jumper's abused joints, not improve a horse's performance. Yet in Marco's case, that's exactly what had happened. Before the therapy, Marco had made few jump-offs. This year he'd only missed two. "I'm sure that's a great possibility if we can make certain he'll be safe. The Olympic Committee won't select them if they see potential medical issues."

"Well, we'll get that all cleared up today."

Not by taking X-rays. Derrick gave a noncommittal nod. "Could you share what's in the herbal treatment? I know you don't think it's related to his behavior, but perhaps in combination with something else he's ingested?"

Cindy picked up the metal film cases and set them aside with her X-ray camera. From her bag, she pulled out a sterile syringe and prepared to take a blood sample. "Well, it's mostly the usual stuff: glucosamine, chondroitin sulfate, tumeric. I've also mixed in several other well-known natural analgesics and anti-inflammatory components like vitamin C, licorice root and devil's claw. But, of course, there are a few secret ingredients." She winked at him, accentuating the word *secret*.

"Anything that could build up over the course of a year?"

"Of course not." She drew the small blood sample from the horse's neck. "I'm not taking blood to look for drugs, if that's what you're thinking. I'm going to check antibodies to see if he needs screening for some other diseases."

Derrick pressed his lips together. "But don't you think you *should* run a drug test on him? We could see if something is mimicking an anabolic steroid in his system."

She eyed him curiously. "How much vet school do you have left, Derrick?"

"A clinic and a couple of classes."

A look of genuine surprise came over her. "That's it?"

"Yes."

"So, almost Dr. Derrick," she said with a grin. "I'm thinking Marco might have something neurological going on. What do you think?"

"It's a possibility." A slim one. Derrick knew that symptoms of neurological disorders usually came on slowly, not overnight. Marco needed a drug screen. If only he could do it himself. For the first time since leaving school, Derrick couldn't wait to get back to his studies and finish. Then, he could take care of Marco the way he saw fit and not have to sit back and watch this lady waste time. Emilie needed this horse declared safe within the next two weeks or he would be of no use to her for the Olympic trials.

Derrick shook his head. What was he thinking? Now that the barn was safe again, he was going back to vet school. And when he finished, he'd have a ministry through horses. So, why was he thinking about Emilie's long-term plans? He wouldn't be around to see them realized.

He dropped his head and sighed. He knew why. And he needed to get over it. Derrick unclipped the horse from the cross ties. "I'll put Marco away and come back to sign your paperwork."

"Meet me at my truck," Cindy said with a coy smile.

Derrick put Marco in his stall, thinking over how to politely opt out of dinner. At the same time, his head filled with questions about Marco and Cindy's therapy. Since he was leaving, he really wanted to know that Marco would be a safe ride for Emilie. He couldn't leave not knowing if she'd be safe.

He doubted he could talk Emilie into calling in another vet for a second opinion so his other option was to talk Cindy into more tests. Find out about more about her therapy. Maybe dinner wasn't such a bad idea after all. Derrick headed to the parking lot. Cindy waited for him beside the truck and handed him a clipboard and a pen. He signed the documents and returned them to her.

"Did you see about dinner?" she asked.

"Yeah. If we make it an early one, I guess it's doable."

"Great." She leaned over and kissed his cheek.

Derrick stiffened at her light touch and caught a stinging whiff of her overly spicy perfume. "Dinner is just dinner. Nothing more."

"Of course." She made a face like he'd been crazy to say such a thing. She climbed into her truck and started the engine. "I'll pick you up here at the stable at six."

"Okay. See you then." He nodded and turned back toward the barn just in time to see Emilie darting through the front doors. His heart froze then crumbled.

No. Oh—no.

Derrick's pulse quickened as he ran after her. If Emilie had witnessed that stupid kiss, there was no telling what she would think. She'd already been frustrated with him for being so standoffish since the kiss. She didn't know he thought of nothing but her, that his arms ached to hold her and his lips burned to kiss her again. And now that James had been arrested, he had to tell her that he'd be leaving. He dreaded it.

They weren't meant to be together. He knew it in his head. His heart seemed to have trouble with the concept.

"Emilie!" Derrick called as he entered the stable. He walked the front section and then the two side wings. No Emilie.

"Emilie!" he called again.

"Here." Her voice sounded dull.

Derrick walked toward the back of the facility. Emilie stood beside what was left of Bugs's stall. He slowed his steps. "We need to talk," he said.

"Well, here I am." She folded her arms across her chest.

"Yes, there you are." Derrick rubbed his temple, staring at her, angry but so beautiful and poised, like the first day he'd met her. What could he say to her? Did it even matter?

After a long silence, she let out a heavy sigh. "When were you going to tell me?"

"Tell you? Tell you what?" Derrick winced. He'd already forgotten about the stupid scene with the vet.

"I just talked to my dad, Derrick." She shot him a look of disgust. "He told me about your conversation in the skybox. I felt so stupid. I had no idea. I hate not knowing what's going on. You should have told me yourself, instead of humiliating me like that."

"Oh, Emilie, I said outrageous things to your father—"

She looked up at him with a spark of hope. "Then you're not leaving?"

Derrick deflated his stance and fell back against the wall for support. His mouth fell open. "Your dad told you I was leaving?"

"I'm sure he would have told me your other surprise, but he probably didn't know you were dating the veterinarian. Did you pretend your back went out to get a kiss from her, too? Or was hers more voluntary?"

"What?" Derrick closed his eyes, shaking his head in disbelief. "Emilie, please. I am not seeing the vet. You can't possibly believe that."

"Interesting that you picked that to deny."

"Well, of course, I'm going to deny it. It's not true. And for the record I didn't ask or want her to kiss me. Beyond finding out what's wrong with your horses, I have no interest in her."

Emilie sneered. "But you are leaving? Before the season's over?"

His stomach lurched. Derrick could barely swallow. How stupid of him to have blurted that news to her father without talking to her first. "I'm sorry you found out that way. I don't blame you for being upset. I was going to tell you. I was just waiting for the details to get worked out so I could explain. And I couldn't leave until I knew you weren't in danger anymore—"

"When?" Emilie spoke low and looked away. "When are you leaving?"

"That's what I'm saying. It depends. I wanted the stable to be safe again—"

"Well, Joyner's arrest took care of that," she snapped back.

"Maybe, Emilie. But they only arrested him for the fire. And really, what could his motive be?"

She crossed her arms over her chest. "You don't

need to worry about that anymore. Mr. Adams says that the police can get Joyner to talk and tell him who was in on it. They think he had a partner."

Derrick shook his head. "I don't know, Emilie. Somehow it just doesn't fit. Joyner? What does he gain by hurting you and Camillo? The stable? I don't feel easy about it."

"And I'm telling you it's not your concern."

"You're telling me not to care? Emilie, I…" He reached out for her hand, but she moved back like his touch would have scalded her. He sighed in frustration. "Then I—I suppose I could leave as soon as you find someone to take over."

"Good, then. I called Mr. Winslow. He already has someone who can be here in a few days. You'll need to train her, but please feel free to leave as soon as she gets the hang of things." She waved her hands in the air to keep him away.

Then, she took another step back. Soft light from the overhead lamp fell across her face. Derrick caught a glimpse of moisture building on her lashes. What could he say to make her understand? He didn't *want* to leave.

She turned slowly and began walking away. A knot formed inside of him and twisted his gut. He couldn't stand watching her go away so hurt because of him.

"Please," he called after her. "Can't I at least have a chance to explain?"

She stopped but kept her back turned to him. "I

already know. My dad says you're going back to school. That's great. Good for you. You'll be a terrific vet." She looked over her shoulder and this time there was no mistaking the tears in her eyes and now on her cheeks. "You probably think I'm overreacting and maybe I am, but I thought we were friends, Derrick. Actually, I thought we were—"

"Emilie, please." He stepped forward.

"No." She held up a hand, indicating for him to stop. "It doesn't matter. I was wrong. I'll get over it."

She took off down the long aisle. Derrick lurched forward, but something deep inside made him stop. *Let her go,* it seemed to say.

"Let her go?" Derrick growled in a low voice. "I don't want to let her go. I want to love her."

TWENTY

Emilie's fingers fiddled with the pearls adorning her neck as she kept watch through the front window for her father's limousine. The pearls had belonged to her mother. As a child, she'd played with them against her mother's soft skin. Touching them now made her ache for her mother and some tender advice. The upsetting conversation with Derrick had left her lonelier than ever.

A long black limousine pulled in front of her home. She turned away from the window, grabbed her clutch bag and scrambled down the front steps as fast as she could. Alan—her father's driver and sometimes bodyguard—held the car door for her.

"Special occasion, Miss Gill?" Alan asked.

"Just dinner I think, but…" She paused, her mouth dropping open. At the far end of the drive, Derrick sat atop Redman, both of them hot and sweaty, out for a vigorous hack. But quickly she straightened her torso, shifting her gaze back to Alan. Derrick didn't deserve her notice, not after he'd crushed her feelings.

"Where to?" she asked the driver.

"Farmington. Your father is already there."

"Perfect." She slipped into the back of the car.

Alan pulled away from the house, passing Derrick and Redman. Through the dark tinted windows, she noticed that he stared after her. He couldn't see inside, but she could clearly see the two long tears that stained his suntanned cheeks.

Well, Derrick's tears meant nothing to her now. He was leaving, just like everyone else she'd ever cared about. But his departure cut deepest because, unlike her mother and Camillo, he had chosen it.

A few minutes later, Emilie held her head high as she glided across the country club dining room.

"You look lovely," her father said as she approached the elegant table. He stood up and kissed her cheek, helping her take a seat.

"Thank you, Daddy." Her eyes turned to the window, which overlooked the club's north lawn, giving way to a spectacular view of the Blue Ridge Mountains as they met the setting sun. "Mother loved this view."

Her father's cheek twitched. His eyes shifted down and away as he took his seat. "Yes, she did. We came here every Wednesday night when you girls were younger."

"I remember." Emilie touched her pearls and swallowed away the lump in her throat. "It has been hard without her."

"I know. And I've been no support to you at all."

"That's not true, Daddy."

"But it is. And we both know it." He grinned at her. "You know you're the spitting image of her. Except for those green eyes. You got those from me. Oh, Emilie, she would have been so proud of you." He reached across the table and squeezed her hand. "I'm proud of you."

Emilie nodded. "Thanks. I needed to hear that." *Especially tonight.*

"I've been too long in saying it." He shook his head. "I don't deserve you. Just like I didn't deserve your mother. The truth is, I'm lost without her."

"It's okay, Dad. Some days, I feel that way, too."

"No, Emilie, it's not okay. I was a terrible husband and an even worse father, especially lately. I've always put work first. Thought there would be time later…now, it's later and she's gone, you and Karin are grown up and I…"

"Just keep working," she said.

He nodded.

"I understand that, Daddy. Sometimes work is the only reason I get up in the morning."

Her father gave her hand a pat then leaned back in his chair and folded his arms across his chest. "Don't try to be like me, Emilie."

"Why not? You're so successful. You built a financial empire from the ground up."

Her father grimaced and signaled the waiter over. "I'll have a Scotch."

"He'll have a seltzer water," Emilie corrected. "Me, too."

The waiter looked confused until her father nodded, then he scurried off to fetch their drinks.

"I know you gave Camillo the cash," she said. "I've known for a while."

He nodded.

"Mr. Adams said it had nothing to do with Camillo's death, but I need to hear it from you. Daddy, why did you pay him? Did you involve him in something illegal? Is that why you've interfered with the police investigation?"

Her father shook his head, closed his eyes and sighed. "No, Emilie. It was never anything like that. The police know about my gifts to Camillo. And regardless of how things might have looked I never stopped the investigation. I just kept the media out of it. Emilie, I hate that Camillo is gone. He treated you like a sister and you needed that. When your mother died, I couldn't be there for you emotionally so I felt like I had to be sure someone else was," he said. "It was payment to assuage my guilt. But, trust me, Camillo would have been there for you anyway. He took the money for his family. He was going to bring them here. It just made me feel better about never being around. It was wrong of me not to tell you. I'm sorry, Emilie."

"And that's it?"

"No…the night your mother died, we were fighting."

"And drinking," she added.

"Yes, but the accident was not your mother's fault. Still, I shouldn't have let her leave the house."

"No, you shouldn't have."

Her father sighed. "Emilie, are you sure you want to hear this?"

"I want to hear the truth."

He nodded. "We were fighting about you. Your mother had learned that Camillo had an affair with that Russian groom who worked for Jack Frahm—"

The blood drained from Emilie's face. Her eyes grew wide. "What? Ivana? And Camillo? Really? I had no idea. Are you sure?"

Her father smirked and took a drink of his water. "I am. And really, it's not that hard to believe. But after that your mother didn't trust him working around you. She didn't like you going to Florida with him unsupervised. And I disagreed."

Emilie swallowed hard. "Why didn't you tell Detective Steele this when he was breathing down my neck about being Camillo's girlfriend?"

"I did." Her father shook his head. "But Camillo wasn't with her anymore. Ivana went back to Russia over a year ago."

"But that note in the Bible, maybe that was to her?"

"When did Camillo start going to church?"

"About six months before he died," she said with a sigh. "So you're right. It wouldn't have been to her." She pressed her lips together. Camillo had had a new girlfriend. But who? "Okay, so Mom didn't trust Camillo but you did?"

"Yes. For one, Camillo feared me and honored you. And I held back his green card and had the power to help him bring his family here. Still, your mother was adamant. She'd found a female groom to take his place. She'd never done anything like that to me. She always trusted my opinions. I don't know why but it hurt me and I completely overreacted.

"When she died that night, I just didn't want anything to do with…"

"With me and the stables," Emilie said, her stomach churning.

"What can I say…I'm a lousy father. I hope one day you can forgive me." He stopped and reached for her hand.

Emilie kept her hand from him. She swallowed down the bile that had crept up her throat and she closed her eyes to shut out the spinning room.

"Emilie, you look ill," her father said. "Let me call Alan. You should go home."

She opened her eyes. "No, Dad. It's just been a long day." *A day of learning that everyone I love has secrets.* She closed her eyes again but it didn't stop her world from spinning round and round.

Her father stood. "I'm calling Alan. You need to go home and rest."

"Yes."

"I'll come with you." Her father checked his watch, just as he always did when he had another appointment.

"No. Don't. I want to be alone." She grabbed her bag and stood.

"But, Emilie, if you need me, I can—"

"Don't promise things you can't deliver." Emilie turned and walked away. Alan and the limo waited just in front of the club. She marched straight to the driver's door.

"Drive me to Warrenton," she told him.

Alan sat up fast and pulled his iPod earbuds away from his head. "Warrenton?"

"Yes. Warrenton. I feel like a little work."

While Alan veered the limousine onto Highway 29, Emilie dug into her bag to find her cell phone. First, she dialed the only three-star hotel near Mr. Winslow's farm and booked a room for the next week. Then she called the trainer to warn him of her early arrival.

"This is good," Mr. Winslow said. "I was thinking of suggesting some extra sessions with Chelsea. Will Derrick be bringing the two mares or should I send Jerome after them?"

"Derrick will be training the new groom," Emilie said. She hated to impose so on Mr. Winslow, but having his groom fetch the horses sounded like a great way to avoid seeing Derrick and that was half of the reason she'd left home.

"I'll call Jerome right now."

"Thank you, Mr. Winslow. I'll have Rosa pack my luggage for him to pick up if that's okay. And be prepared—I'm ready to work harder than I ever have in my life."

"Not to fear, Miss Gill. I'll keep you busy."

Derrick had one goal in mind while eating dinner with Cindy and that was to discover her plan for treating Emilie's horses—in particular, Marco. He couldn't leave Cedar Oaks without knowing Emilie and her horses were safe and in good hands.

But focusing the conversation proved hard work. Cindy didn't seem the least bit interested in talking shop. Every time he asked a question about her treatment plan she steered the conversation to another topic.

And Derrick was having troubles of his own focusing. It was hard to talk horses when all he could think of was Emilie. Watching her glide down the front steps in that stunning cocktail dress had nearly brought him to his knees. She moved with such elegance, every look and gesture confirming her comfort and ease with the world of wealth she lived in. Who was he to think she might consider him?

And yet, it had crossed her mind. She'd said so. Not in so many words, but she had admitted to sensing the connection between them. The fact she was so upset about his leaving meant she had some sort of feelings for him. He couldn't fault her for running off. He should have talked to her first about his plans, not last. He had only himself to blame for that. And no matter how he told her, the end result would still be the same. He had to leave.

Derrick shook his head, trying to erase the constant image of Emilie from his mind. "Were you able to run any of Marco's tests? Develop X-rays?"

Cindy again looked annoyed. "Sure. The X-rays were clean. The blood, I sent to a lab. I'll call you when I hear back. But, tell me about you. What are your plans?"

"I'll be heading back to school."

"Really." She looked pleased now. "I'd love to see your résumé when you pass boards. I'm looking for a partner."

"I'll keep that in mind," he said, even though he had his own plan, his direction from God that he'd prayed for, for so long. Nothing he wanted to discuss with Cindy Saunders. "Now about Marco. I'm thinking his behavior yesterday was similar to Duchess when—"

"Yes, of course," she interrupted. "We'll compare blood samples if we need to. Trust me. I'll take care of Marco."

Derrick gritted his teeth.

"Tell me more about the arrest," she added. "You hardly said a word earlier."

Good grief. By now, Cindy probably knew more than he did about it. It was just another way to change the subject. "I told you all I know. They connected James to the fire and they arrested him."

"But you were there, right? What did he say?"

"James? He stayed quiet. Kept his head down." Derrick shook his head, remembering the moment. "Honestly, I can't make heads or tails of it. I can't see what Joyner would have had to gain by setting fire to Emilie's stable."

"Well, I always found him a bit strange. He did great work, though. Folks around here will be scrambling for a new farrier."

"Strange or not, there had to be some sort of reason for what he did," Derrick said.

"What do you mean? You don't think he did it?" Cindy looked intrigued.

Derrick shrugged. "I didn't say that. It just seems like only half the story to me."

Cindy smiled. "So, you're a vet and a sleuth?"

"Actually, I'm a student and a groom. But I don't think it takes any sort of special skills to suspect that all the strange events at the stable are related. Which is why I'm going to keep pushing for you to conduct a drug test on Emilie's horses."

"But we know what her horses take. It would be a waste of time."

"Someone broke in and mixed dangerous amphetamines in her horses' electrolytes. I don't think it's so crazy after Marco's behavior yesterday to wonder if someone tried that again and succeeded."

Cindy pushed her plate aside. "You really just came out tonight to talk about horses, didn't you?"

Derrick nodded slowly. "Yes, I did. I'm worried about them. And about Emilie."

"I'm sorry to hear that." Cindy gave a half smile. "I think we came here with different expectations."

"Then, perhaps we should call it a night," Derrick said. The sooner he could get back to the estate the sooner he could find Emilie and talk to her.

By the time Emilie reached Peter Winslow's, her stomach had clenched tighter than a sailor's knot. She'd acted childishly with her father. She shouldn't have run off. Sure, it had been hard to hear the truth, but at least he was telling it. Her father had tried. He wasn't perfect, but he tried in his own way. So, why had she run off? What was frightening her? The truth about Camillo? Derrick's leaving? Or something else altogether?

Alan held the door to the limo open. She slid out of the back and stared up at the front steps of the cabin. Her heart beat slow and heavy against her ribs. Why had she come here? Suddenly, she wished she were anywhere else.

"Wait a few minutes, please," she told the driver. "I don't think I'll be long."

Alan nodded.

Emilie scurried up the steps to the cabin door and knocked cautiously.

"Good evening, Miss Gill. You arrived quickly."

Mr. Winslow glanced at the limousine then back to Emilie, lifting an eyebrow. "Come inside."

He escorted her into the living area.

Emilie glanced nervously around the small room. A room she'd once thought cozy and quaint. Tonight, it felt stuffy and confining.

"I sent Jerome for your horses as you requested," he said. "He'll bring Duchess and Chelsea."

"Yes. Derrick would be upset if I brought Marco." *Derrick*. Her breath caught in her throat. She clenched her teeth and tried to compose her rattled nerves. "Thank you. I left in a hurry. I…" She smiled and shrugged, searching for some explanation for her unexpected arrival. "I feel that I've imposed. I'm sorry, Mr. Winslow. I'll just—"

"Don't be silly." The older man smiled and directed her to the couch. "How about a cup of tea?"

She nodded and took a seat while her trainer disappeared to the kitchen. The longer he took to fix the tea, the more Emilie wanted to leave. After a few minutes of feeling her heart beat against her chest like a drum, she stood and started for the door.

"Do you need to fetch something from the limousine?" Mr. Winslow returned with a loaded tray and began to serve.

"No, sir. I—" Emilie shook her head. "I'm just feeling out of sorts this evening. Perhaps I should go on to the hotel. I might be coming down with something."

"And waste a perfectly good cup of tea? Please."

He gestured again to the couch. "It's early yet. As you see, I have nothing planned this evening. Miss Gill, it's easy to see you have something on your mind. You'll find I'm an excellent listener."

"Oh no. I'm fine. Just came here to work," she said, knowing as the words came out that they weren't the least bit true. But why did she come here?

Mr. Winslow raised an eyebrow. "Really? Because I'm guessing it has nothing to do with horses at all. Does it?"

Emilie's heart raced as she took her seat again on the couch. "I could make it about the horses." She laughed nervously. "At least, I'd know what I was talking about. But you're right. For once I feel like horses and work aren't going to be enough. This is going to sound stupid, Mr. Winslow, but all the time I feel this tugging inside of me. And I don't know why or what to do about it. I thought it was stress about the Olympic trials but my points are high. I'll make the trials no matter what now. So that can't be it." She looked up at him. "I'm not making any sense, am I?"

Mr. Winslow smiled. "Perhaps you have spiritual questions. That tugging you feel, maybe it's a desire to understand your relationship with God."

Again, the urge to flee seized her. The walls seemed to move in closer. Fear grew inside her belly. "I don't know," she said. "I don't understand God. I've tried, but He asks me to accept a friend's sense-less death, a mother killed in a car accident and a father who's never around. And yet I'm supposed to believe that He loves me?"

Mr. Winslow reached across the coffee table between them and patted her hand. "You won't understand everything in this life. But that doesn't change the fact that God loves you. He's there for you and He wants you to seek Him. That's the tugging, Emilie. And you won't find peace until you accept it."

Peace. The peace Derrick and her sister and Mr. Winslow had. That could be hers? "I want to believe that, Mr. Winslow. I do."

"Then maybe it's time to stop asking questions and just make a decision," he said.

It sounded so simple. Emilie nodded, taking a couple of short breaths. Maybe it was that simple. Maybe she was the complication. Her heart lifted. "Yes. That's it," she said, shutting out the fear in her mind. "That's what I need to do."

Mr. Winslow nodded and gave her hand a squeeze. "Then let's say a little prayer together, shall we?"

And as Mr. Winslow began to speak, tears of tension and bitterness rolled out and down her cheeks. And peace flowed in.

TWENTY-ONE

"Here's my number." Cindy handed Derrick a business card. "You should call in a few months when you're looking for a job."

Derrick hesitated then took the card. "Right. I'll be in touch about Marco."

He climbed out of the car quickly and closed the door, surprised to find lights on in the stable. Before he'd left, he'd turned them off and set the alarms. Maybe Emilie was there? He took a shallow breath and hurried inside.

"Hello?" Derrick called down the front aisle. "Emilie?"

His eyes swept over the front three stalls. Empty. Marco would still be in the front paddock. But where were Duchess and Chelsea? Before dinner, he'd brought them inside and fed them. They couldn't have gotten out. Their stalls were barred. Panic gripped Derrick's lungs.

Loud sounds from the west gate echoed through the stable. Derrick busted around the corner, but came to a screeching halt as he nearly mowed over Emilie's father. "Mr. Gill?"

"Randall." Emilie's father wiped a finger across his mustache. His lips formed a scowl. "Why aren't *you* taking Emilie's horses to Winslow's?"

Derrick glanced down to the end of the aisle. Peter's trailer was backed up to the west doors. Jerome, Peter's stable hand, was latching up the loaded trailer.

"I didn't know anything about this." Derrick stood with his mouth half open. "Where is Emilie?"

Mr. Gill let out a heavy sigh. "I don't know. She left the club upset with me. I was looking for her here. She's not answering her cell."

Derrick studied the man's eyes. For once, he saw a parent's honest worry in them. "She's upset with me, too."

Mr. Gill's expression softened further. "That's my fault, I suppose. I didn't know you hadn't told Emilie that you had decided to leave."

"So, she went to Peter's." Derrick tried not to sound too disappointed. He shifted his weight nervously, looking around the stable.

"It appears so." Mr. Gill's cheek twitched. "At least, she'll get there safely. She's with Alan."

Derrick nodded. "I could call Peter."

"If she wanted to talk, she'd answer her cell or she'd be here." Mr. Gill held out his hand. "Good luck to you. I didn't think your leaving would come so easy."

Derrick frowned and didn't take Mr. Gill's hand. "It didn't."

Mr. Gill dropped his hand and walked off toward the entrance. He paused at the corner and looked back over his shoulder. "We haven't agreed on much, Randall. But I approve of your leaving. My daughter is not for you."

"Wouldn't that be for her to decide?" Derrick uttered the words before he could stop himself. He already wished them back.

"She made her decision," Mr. Gill said. "She even hired a new groom."

Derrick clenched his teeth as he watched Mr. Gill head out of the stable. He shook his head, feeling the angry heat rise to his cheeks. He had no right to feel the way he did. Mr. Gill was right. Emilie wasn't for him. Didn't make hearing it any easier.

The west gate closed and the muffled sounds of gravel churning under Peter's trailer came through the walls of the stable. Derrick's whole body tensed with frustration. Now he would never get to talk to Emilie. If going back to school was the right decision, why did he feel so horrible? He wanted to hit something. Anything. He wanted to destroy something the way he felt his heart had been destroyed. Derrick paced through the stable, stopping in front of Bugs's old burnt up stall. He kicked at a charred section of the wall. Most of the panel broke and crumbled to the ground, all but one small piece hanging there in defiance. Derrick kicked it again, this time his foot sticking between the studs.

"Great," he mumbled. "Stupid barn." *Stupid me.*

He slipped his foot from the boot, grabbed the shoe with his hands and yanked. The boot and the board came loose, sending Derrick to his backside. He stood, humiliated, then bent closer to look inside the wall. There was something there. He reached his hands between the studs and wrapped his fingers around the object. It was a book—a book in the wall of the stable. And not just any wall. In the wall of the stallion's stall. Bugs had always been Emilie's favorite and most valuable horse. As he opened the book, Derrick saw that it was a personal ledger, like an accountant might use. Quickly, he slipped his boot back on and moved under a strong light to have a closer look.

The pages had been browned some by smoke, but the handwritten entries remained legible. Three columns per page, all recorded in the same fashion. First, dates. Then, a group of letters. And in the final column…numbers, like…

Derrick shook his head. Could it be?

Faster and faster, Derrick turned the pages, every entry only confirming his idea that each letter corresponded to the stall of a particular horse. The numbers seemed to indicate some sort of measurement. Maybe a dosage.

Derrick stuck the book under his arm then pulled out his cell to dial Peter.

A little white paper slipped from the logbook to the floor. As Peter's phone went to voice mail, Derrick picked up the note.

Emilie,
I didn't know what was in the vials at first. I didn't know what she was asking me to do. I hope you'll find it in your heart to forgive me. And do what you must. I don't deserve to be protected.
Your friend always, Camillo

Derrick placed the note back inside the logbook and canceled the call to Peter. Then with his thumb, he searched his caller list for Detective Steele's number.

Emilie spun the pearls on the necklace again. The ride home from Winslow's seemed to take forever. Part of her hadn't wanted to leave. It would have been easy to spend a few more days with Mr. Winslow, hiding away and growing in her decision for Christ. But right now, she needed to finish the conversation with her father, and the conversation with Derrick— she hoped she would be brave enough to tell them everything. And to listen. She shouldn't have walked away from either of them.

The limousine turned into the estate and headed up the long hill to her house. As they rolled past the stable road, Emilie noticed a glow in the night sky. The lights must have still been on in the stable. Maybe Jerome was just arriving? Or perhaps Derrick was there?

"Alan, take me to the stable," she said.

"Sure." He turned the big vehicle around and headed to the stable.

Derrick's car alone sat in front. Emilie smiled and hopped out of the limo before Alan could open the door for her. "I'll catch a ride to the house with Derrick. Good night, Alan. And thanks."

She stood on the front porch for a moment, nervous about facing Derrick and at the same time anxious to see him. With a deep breath, she pushed through the front doors of the stable, heading to her office first. Halfway across the aisle, a deafening blast erupted through the air. Emilie crouched to the ground, looking in every direction, her heartbeat thumping in her ears. Horses whinnied and kicked. Then, the stable went dark. A complete blackout.

"Put the phone down on the ground."

Derrick stiffened at the sound of Cindy Saunders's voice. Slowly, he lowered his arm and dropped the phone to the ground.

"Easy," she said. "Keep your hands out to your sides and turn around. I have a gun."

Derrick lifted his arms away from his body and turned slowly toward her voice. Cindy stood in the aisle, legs planted, aiming a large automatic pistol at his head.

"Who did you call?" she asked nervously. "What's that in your hand?"

"I didn't call anyone." Derrick tried to keep his voice steady. He forced himself to take some deep breaths but it wasn't so pleasant looking down the wrong end of a firearm. "Why the gun, Cindy? You want to talk? I'll talk to you. Put the gun down." He made a subtle move forward.

"Get back. You had your chance to talk at dinner," she growled. "Now you're going to listen."

"That's fine. I can listen. What's wrong?" Like he didn't already know.

"You. That's what's wrong. I got halfway home and realized that you would talk Emilie into ordering that drug test on Marco. She'd do anything you said. It was like that with Camillo, but I could control Camillo. But you! You think you're a real vet. Well, let me tell you something. You don't have any idea what it's like to vet horses worth millions of dollars that suddenly lose their value due to something out of your control. People hold you responsible. You'll see. Maybe. Now, put the book down and slide it to me."

Derrick placed the book on the floor and slid it over to where she stood. She flicked the cover open with the toe of her shoe and glanced down.

"Finally." She tossed her head back and chuckled low in her throat. "You just found this, didn't you?"

Derrick didn't bother to reply. He stared her in the eyes and stripped his face of all emotion.

"This is Camillo's log. I've been looking everywhere for it. I set the barn on fire just on the off chance that it might get destroyed wherever Camillo had hidden it. Perfect. Now I just need Duchess and Marco. Where are they?" she sneered. She stepped on the book, grinding it into the cement.

Derrick watched her every movement, hoping for a chance to rush at her. But she stood too far away. He needed to get her closer. He turned around, looking for something to distract her with.

"Quit moving unless I tell you to or you're going to end up like Camillo." She cocked the gun and moved closer, now pointing the barrel at his chest. "Where are the horses?"

Derrick closed his eyes. He had to stall her. Think of something to do or say. She couldn't get away with that book or have access to Emilie's horses. "What horses?" he said.

"Very funny." She kicked the book into the wall then stepped wide around him so that she and the gun stood behind him. "You know, I'm not a little rich princess like Emilie. I know how to use this gun."

Derrick felt the barrel of the gun press between his shoulder blades.

"Keep your arms out and tell me where the horses are."

"Right…um…Duchess is gone."

"Where?" she screamed.

Derrick could tell her patience had run thin. "On her way to…" Not to Winslow's, he thought. "To a potential buyer. Somewhere in New York." It was a lie, but it might keep the horse, Peter and Jerome safe.

Cindy cursed then fell silent for what seemed like an eternity.

Please, Lord, keep me brave, keep me strong, keep me Yours. And guide me. Derrick steadied his breathing, the gun still at his back.

"What about Marco?"

Derrick swallowed hard. Marco was in the paddock, but he didn't want to tell her that. He tried to think of another idea. Something to stall her. Cindy pressed the gun into his back again.

"He's here."

She laughed. "Lead me to him. But first pick up that book. We have to get rid of it, too."

Derrick walked slowly to the book, his arms out to his sides. He kneeled to the floor and reached for the book. Then with a quick move, he grabbed it and threw it at Cindy's face. At the same time, he dived to the other side of the aisle, out of her line of fire.

The blast of the gun exploded through the stable. A ping sounded as the bullet ricocheted off the concrete aisle. A sharp stinging pricked into the back of Derrick's calf. But he didn't stop. The feed room was only ten feet away and there, the electrical panel for the stable. Cindy stood behind him, regaining her balance. She cocked and lifted the gun again.

Quick! Derrick pulled open the metal door to the electrical panel, flipped the main switch and ducked.

TWENTY-TWO

A second blast echoed through the dark stable. This time, there was no mistaking the sound of gunfire.

"Derrick!" Emilie screamed.

Panic grew inside her, racing through her limbs and prickling over her skin. *God is with me. God is with me,* she chanted to herself. *And with Derrick. Please. Please don't let him be hurt.* She couldn't bear to lose him, too.

"Emilie, get out of the stable! Run!" Derrick's deep voice reverberated through the aisles and off the concrete floors, flooding her ears from all angles. She couldn't tell where he was.

The sounds of gunfire combined with the inky black interior of the stable terrorized the horses. Neighs, nickers and kicks echoed off the walls. Emilie knew Derrick couldn't have fired those shots. Was someone trying to shoot him? Had they succeeded? Her ears strained to hear above the animal din.

Before panic could take hold, she shook the thought from her head. *Peace. And faith.* With a deep breath, she reached into her handbag, pulled out her phone and dialed nine-one-one.

"Shots fired at Cedar Oaks Stable. 16400 Old Mill Lane. Hurry," she whispered.

A shoe scuffed across the floor.

Someone was close. Too close.

Her heart pounding, she ended the call and hid the light of the touch-screen phone against her chest. She slipped off her dress shoes and made her way to the wall in front of her office then inched her way along toward the front doors. Derrick had told her to leave. But what if he needed her? What if he'd been hurt? And the police might take a while to get there. Unless a squad car happened to be nearby, the estate was a good twenty minutes from town. She couldn't just leave him there.

"You can hand that phone to me now."

Emilie froze then turned toward the familiar voice. Cindy Saunders stepped forward from the darkness, a long firearm in her hands.

"You didn't think I would find you with the light on that thing? It's like a beacon in here," Cindy said, holding one hand out.

Cindy? Emilie held the phone out and blinked at her as the pieces fell into place. *It's about the horses.* Hector Emens's words. Flashes of Camillo and Cindy laughing together. Camillo's insistence on keeping Cindy as the equine vet after the controversy with her therapy. The horses' strange behavior in between "therapy" treatments. Camillo's secret, it was with Cindy.

"Hand it over," the vet ordered.

"What have you done?" Emilie held the phone out to her.

Cindy snatched it from her hand, turned off the power and threw the device across the aisle. It crashed against the opposite wall. Blackness coated the space once again. Something cold and hard pressed into her temple. Emilie didn't need a light to know Cindy had pressed the gun to her head. She whimpered as the barrel pushed harder against her skull.

"Move to your office," Cindy ordered her.

Emilie stepped slowly back, her legs trembling, barely supporting her weight. "Where's Derrick? Did you—did you shoot him?"

"Open the office," Cindy growled.

"I don't have the key with me."

"Why do you need to get in the office?" Derrick's voice sounded from the dark.

Cindy kept the gun pressed against Emilie's temple. "I've got your princess at the end of my gun. If I were you, I wouldn't try any superhero moves."

"Derrick, it's true." Emilie's voice trembled. "But I'm okay. And I called the police."

"Good girl," Derrick said. This time, his voice came from yet another direction.

"Enough," Cindy shouted. "I'll shoot her. And I know you don't want that."

"Of course, I don't want that. Why do you need to get in the office? I thought you wanted Marco," Derrick answered.

"You know as well as I do that there's another panel for the lights inside." Cindy cocked the gun. Emilie whimpered as Cindy jabbed it now into the back of her neck.

"Take it easy, Cindy. I have a key," Derrick said. "I left it on the front table for you."

"You pick it up." Cindy pressed Emilie with the gun toward the long table situated near the door to her office.

Emilie ran her shaking hands across the surface until her fingers found the key. "Got it."

A light spotted in their direction. Emilie turned. It was a flashlight from Marco's stall. Derrick had probably grabbed the one from the feed room. It lit the space around her and Cindy, flashing directly on Cindy's face, right in her eyes. Cindy cursed and looked back to step out of the bright beam. Unguarded, Emilie took her chance and pushed the vet as hard as she could.

"Run, Emilie." Derrick's voice boomed through the entranceway.

He was close, his command uttered from just a few feet behind her. She trusted his words and sprinted away. The light from the flashlight helped to guide her past the stalls of the north wing. Her bare feet padded over the concrete. Behind her, Derrick and

Cindy struggled. Emilie heard jumbled words and quick movements. Another shot fired.

Emilie stopped and turned. She had to go back and help somehow. If it wasn't too late. In the dim light, she searched along the outside of the stalls for something to give her some leverage—a rake, a pitchfork, a length of rope, anything. Maybe in the wash stall? She moved into the open wash area, feeling her way along the wall to the back corner, slowing her steps as the space grew darker and darker. Her eyes slowly adjusted to the change in the lighting as she left the stream of light provided by the flashlight. She reached out for the rake hanging on the hook above the hoses.

"Just what do you need that rake for?" A hand from the darkness wrapped tightly around her upper arm and forced her to the corner of the wash stall. The voice was all too familiar.

"Jack," Emilie gasped. "What are you—?"

"Good night, Emilie." Something hard came down on her neck. Pain riveted through her body and she slumped to the ground.

Derrick moved in behind the vet and batted her hand. The pistol fell to the floor. Cindy scrambled after it. Derrick pushed her to the side, grabbed her left arm and twisted it high behind her back.

She uttered a cry of pain as he lifted her to her feet again.

"I'd let go if I were you," she said.

"No, thanks. I think we'll just stay like this until the police get here." He lifted the twisted arm higher, up toward her shoulders.

"Think again." Cindy raised her other arm. The pistol clicked in her fingers.

Derrick released her, but not without giving her a great shove toward the front doors. While she regained her balance, Derrick grabbed the flashlight from Marco's stall and clicked it off, surrounding them in darkness. Then he carefully moved in the direction of the feed room.

Fumbling his way back along the stalls, he dropped to the floor. He had to find that logbook. Then he'd catch up with Emilie, who he hoped had slipped out the west gate. Panting for air, aching from the shot in his leg, he grazed his hands across the concrete in a rush, expecting Cindy and her gun would follow at any second. Angry words sounded from the entrance.

"We'll leave as soon as I get that logbook." Cindy's voice rang through the silent barn. Apparently, she hadn't come after him. She was still at the entrance.

"Forget the book," a man said. "Little Miss Gill called the police."

"Do what you want, Jack! I'm not leaving without the book," Cindy said.

Jack? Jack Frahm? What is he doing here? Derrick's fingers touched the side of the book.

"Fine. You find the book," Jack said. "I'll find Randall."

"What about Emilie?"

"I took care of her."

Emilie? What did he do to Emilie? Rage flooded through Derrick's veins as he snatched the logbook from the floor and moved quickly toward the north wing, the direction he knew Emilie had run in.

"Emilie?" he whispered into the stalls as he passed, wondering if she could even answer him. A few neighs and whinnies responded to his whisper but nothing more. He reached the wash stalls at the end of the aisle. Where was she? What had Jack done to her?

Derrick made his way across the open wash stall, feeling his way along the wall. His foot thunked into something solid on the rubber mat. A moan ensued.

Dear Lord! Derrick fell to his knees and reached in front of him. A leg. Emilie's leg. She was lying facedown on the rubber mat. But she'd moaned. She had to be alive.

Thank You, Lord! He rolled her to her back. His pulse throbbed.

"Emilie. Are you okay? I need to move you."

"Derrick?"

Speaking. That was good. Still, Jack would pay for this. Derrick stuck the book on her belly and scooped her into his arms, wondering where he could take her out of harm's way. He stepped into the aisle again.

A loud click sounded overhead. The barn flooded with light. Cindy or Jack had found the power box.

"It's not there." Cindy's anger reverberated through the now brightly lit stable. "Randall's got it. Find him and hurry. I'm going to get to work on Marco. He must be in the front paddock."

Derrick stared down at Emilie, lying limp in his arms. A rush of emotions flowed through his veins. The same ones he felt every time she was near. Every time he watched her ride. Every time her hand brushed against his. "You okay? Did he hurt you?"

"I'm fine. Just sore. He hit me in the neck." She squinted under the bright light.

Derrick nodded then looked up and down the aisle. There was no time to get to a door. Instead, he slid into the nearest stall with her. Panda, the paint pony who lived there, came over and gave them a sniff. Derrick laid Emilie in a clean spot in the bedding and crouched beside her.

"I have something to tell you." She looked up at him with those emerald eyes that had long ago stolen his heart.

"Shh. Just be still." He touched a hand to her soft cheek.

"I did it," she said. "I prayed."

Derrick paused a moment, letting the meaning behind her words register. Could it be true? He hardly dared believe. Too much of his own happiness rested on this. *Is it possible, Lord?*

Derrick smiled at her and shook his head. No. She

must have been hit hard and didn't know what she was saying. "You're sure you're okay?"

"Never been better." She grabbed his hand and gave it a squeeze. "Honest. I love God. I think I always have. I just didn't know what to do with it, you know? Didn't get the trust part of things."

Her words pierced his heart, hotter than the bullet that had grazed his leg. All his prayers for her, all his hope, even his own struggles and heartache of wanting what he thought to be impossible, all worth the pain and efforts. Worth the pleasure and happiness of arriving at this moment.

"Oh, Emilie." Derrick lowered his head and gave her a soft kiss on the mouth. Another on the forehead. He took in a deep breath, memorizing every detail of her face and eyes and smile. "Soon, we can talk about all this."

She nodded.

"How long for the police?"

"Maybe another five to ten minutes," she whispered.

"That's too long. Too long for Marco." Derrick stood and listened for Jack and Cindy.

"You're bleeding!" Emilie reached up and touched his calf. "We should just leave and get you help." She pressed up from the ground.

"It's just a graze. Burns like crazy but I'm fine." He touched his hand to her head to stop her from standing.

"You sure?" She dropped her hand and it fell to the logbook beside her in the bedding. "What's this?"

Derrick knelt again beside her. "It's what Camillo left you. Your evidence against Cindy." He flipped the book open to the letter. "They've been doping your horses. Probably with equine steroids."

Emilie's expression remained surprisingly calm as her eyes grazed over the note from Camillo. He noticed a calm, true peace about her. "Where did you find this?"

Derrick pressed his lips together, thinking about how he'd kicked the stall in frustration. "How about I explain that later? Right now, they've got Marco."

The sound of hooves clippity-clopping across the front of the stable reached their ears. Derrick peeked out of the pony's stall. Cindy led the large gelding in, Jack at her side with the gun.

Emilie stood and peered out of the stall. "What are they going to do to him? They're going to hurt him, aren't they?"

"No." Derrick turned to her and framed her face in his hands. "They're not. I'm going to stop them."

TWENTY-THREE

"How? He's got a gun and she..." Emilie twisted her hands together as she and Derrick peered toward Jack and Cindy. "What do you think she's going to do to Marco? And how was she doping them? They have regular urine checks. None of this makes sense, Derrick."

"I know it doesn't all fit together yet. And I don't know how the doping hasn't been detected. But right now I know she's giving something to Marco that at the very least will keep him from being ridden again."

Emilie gasped. "She's going to kill him?"

"She's probably going to give him a huge dose of amphetamines. Enough to send him into cardiac arrest. I'll need to distract Jack. Slow them down somehow until the police get here."

"Well, you can't just go running down the aisle," she said. "Jack has a gun."

"Right." Derrick looked around the space. Then he turned his head up, his eyes on the rafters. "You got enough strength to give me a leg up?"

Emilie smiled and clasped her fingers together, bracing herself for his weight. Derrick stepped into her hands with a mighty leap upward and she lifted him the extra bit so that his hands reached the wooden rails over the stall.

With care, Derrick shimmied up and onto the structural beams framing the stable. Then he crawled across the support rafters, slowly making his way to the area above the entrance and Marco's stall. Jack Frahm paced underneath him, waiting for Cindy to finish her work.

"Come on," Jack bellowed. "Why is this taking so long? We need to get out of here."

"Why don't you go look for Randall and that book? Like I asked you to," Cindy said. "I've got to mix the masking agent. It'll just be a minute."

A masking agent? Emilie shook her head and leaned back against the stall. That's how her horses had been able to pass the routine urine tests. But for the Olympics, the testing was much more rigorous. Cindy knew that. She couldn't risk Emilie making it through the trials. That's why she'd done all of this. Cindy was willing to risk everything—including Emilie's life—to save her own reputation.

The stable grew quiet. Emilie gazed around the corner again.

Derrick hung motionless in the rafters above where Jack walked in a quick circle. He waited for just the right second then he slipped from the high beam down onto Jack.

Emilie held in a gasp and leaned back against the stall again, closing her eyes. *Lord, I'm kind of new at this but could You keep Derrick safe? Please.*

Emilie heard the struggle between Derrick and Jack and peeked back around the corner. The gun had fallen away. Derrick and Jack took swings at each other. Jack missed. Derrick pushed Jack to the floor, subdued him and wrestled his arms behind his back.

Cindy had taken Marco to his stall and locked him in. But the gun still lay on the floor, too far for Derrick to reach, and now Cindy approached.

Emilie's heart froze, but it was too late. Cindy was headed for the gun. Emilie had no chance to get there before her. But she had to do something.

Cindy grabbed the gun. "Give us the book, Randall, and we'll leave."

Marco, already reacting to whatever Cindy had given him, emitted distressing whinnies. Derrick clambered to his feet, holding Jack Frahm in front of him with one arm still twisted behind his back.

"Don't think I won't shoot just because you're holding Jack. I killed Camillo, who I liked a lot better than him," Cindy smirked.

Cindy had killed Camillo. Emilie wanted to be sick right there.

"But you need him. Need his horses to keep promoting your therapy," Derrick said to Cindy. He was stalling her. Using up the seconds until the police could arrive. "Isn't that right?"

He took tiny steps around the vet until he and Jack disappeared from her view behind the wall of the office. Cindy now had her back toward Emilie. Marco continued to cry and pace. He kicked the walls and bit the bars to the stall.

Emilie slipped from Panda's stall unnoticed and made her way toward Cindy. She wasn't sure what she could do though. She couldn't risk Cindy shooting at Jack and Derrick.

"Actually, she doesn't need me anymore," Jack said. "I funded her research for the masking agent but it still won't pass the top testing. So, really she'd be better off without me. Isn't that right?"

"Don't tempt me." Cindy waved the gun.

Emilie continued to scurry down the aisle. So close now. The logbook in her hands.

"Get me that book, Randall."

"You mean this book?" Emilie said.

Cindy flinched but stopped herself from turning to Emilie. She knew that if she did Derrick would have the chance to attack her. "I wouldn't come any closer if I were you, Emilie."

"Then it's going to be pretty hard for you to get this book from me." Emilie took another step forward.

"Stay right there." Cindy waved the gun. "Let Jack get it."

Marco let out another distressing blast. He reared and crashed down against the stall door.

"What did you do to him?"

"Nothing. Just a little insurance so you won't take him to trials. Now, give Jack the book."

"Jack is staying right here," said Derrick.

Sirens sounded in the distance. The police had entered the estate. Only a minute or two now.

"There's no way out of here, Cindy," Emilie said. "It's over. Put the gun down."

Cindy's calm facade began to crumble. She started to back away, her hands shaking. Marco fussed again and kicked the door.

"Toss me the book, Emilie."

The sirens grew louder.

"Now!" Cindy screamed.

Emilie swung the book at her with an easy toss. She didn't want Cindy firing the gun accidentally, trying to catch the book. The vet snatched the book from the air. She laughed, undid the snap latch on Marco's stall and ran through the front doors.

Derrick shoved Jack to the ground. Emilie ran toward Marco's stall. "Look at him. Whatever she gave him is already taking effect."

The large horse thrashed against the side of his stall again.

"Don't, Emilie. It's not safe." Derrick stepped forward ready to stop her.

She ignored him and raced to the door. "Get some calming paste."

"Just wait, Emi—"

The gelding snorted and backed into the far corner. Just as she reached the main latch to the door, he charged. She did what she could to get out of his way, but he clipped her. She went down on the concrete floor, seeing nothing but long black legs around her. Emilie tried to slither away. But a hard, sharp hoof pinned her to the floor. Pain shattered through her body. Her lungs tightened. She closed her eyes and rolled to her side.

She could hear Derrick emitting a loud "whoop" and Marco scrambling away. Poor horse. He didn't know what he'd done. The pain grew more intense, bursting from her spine out to her limbs. She groaned and gasped for her breath.

"Stay with me." Derrick's voice said to her. She felt him around her. "You're going to be fine. Everything's going to be fine."

TWENTY-FOUR

Derrick sat in the hospital waiting area between Karin and Max. Peter was there, too, standing near the doors to the E.R. Mr. Gill had been the only one summoned inside by the surgeon. Derrick knew that couldn't be a good sign. Carrying her to the ambulance, there'd been so much blood.

"I don't get it." Max shook his head. "Why would the vet dope Emilie's horses? I kind of get Jack doing it, but not the vet."

Derrick lifted his head, but his mind was still back at the stable where Emilie had been taken in the ambulance. Detective Steele had stopped Cindy. She'd still had the logbook. He'd arrested both her and Jack for murder and arson. James would be released. He'd had nothing to do with any of it—aside from being Cindy's lover after Camillo had ended things. Cindy's access to James's house had made it easy for her to steal his space heater, and plant evidence.

Derrick cleared his throat and turned to Max. "The joint therapy that made Cindy an overnight success in veterinarian medicine had never been properly tested. This happens sometimes. Paperwork doesn't get done and things that shouldn't get pushed ahead. So, while the equine world is going crazy over this stuff, Cindy learns that its effects only last for six months and then actually begin to deteriorate cartilage. By this time she's already making millions off the formula."

"Yes, but people will stop using it when it stops working, right?" Karin said.

"Not when riders like Emilie and Jack endorse it."

Max groaned. "So she just had to keep Jack and Emilie thinking that it worked. Keep their faces on her ads in *Horse World* and she would keep making millions."

"Emilie's the only one she really had to fool. Jack played along for a share of the profits, but they both knew Emilie was too honest to do the same. So she doped Emilie's horses and with Jack's help, developed a masking agent so that the steroids wouldn't show in a urine test," Derrick explained.

"But Marco and Bugs were jumping so well that Emilie was easily going to trials with both of them. The testing is more rigorous there and the drugs would have been detected."

"Well, why didn't she just quit doping them altogether?" Karin asked.

"Because then the horses wouldn't jump well and at best, she'd lose Emilie as an endorser. At worst Emilie would realize the horses were going through withdrawal and get them tested before the drugs were fully out of their systems. And either way, Cindy couldn't lose Emilie's support for the treatment. Emilie is golden in the hunter/jumper world. Whatever she does, every little girl with a pony wants to do."

"That's right," Peter said with a smile. "Just think of the witness she can be now."

Derrick wanted to share Peter's enthusiasm, but he couldn't. Not without seeing her first. Knowing she was okay. He stood from his chair and paced the short space in front of Max and Karin. "You didn't see her," he said. "Marco crushed her. When they took her away, she couldn't move from the waist down. I've been sitting here trying to imagine Emilie without riding in her life and I...I just can't do it."

"Mr. Randall?" a nurse called from the E.R. doors.

Derrick spun around.

"Miss Gill is asking for you."

Derrick's heartbeat throbbed in his ears as he followed the nurse past the E.R. and through the intensive care unit. She stopped at door number 3. Derrick could hear Mr. Gill's voice inside the doors, but not Emilie's.

"Go ahead," the nurse said.

Derrick took a deep breath and promised to be brave no matter what Emilie had to face, no matter how much it tore him apart.

"Randall." Mr. Gill held out a hand.

Derrick shook his hand but his eyes focused on Emilie. She lay there, eyes closed, pale and fragile as ever, tubes running all around her arms.

"I think she just went back to sleep," Mr. Gill said.

"No," Emilie said in a hoarse voice. "I'm awake." She looked at Derrick. "Can we talk?"

Derrick nodded. Emilie looked back to her father. "Can you give us a few minutes, Daddy?"

"Sure. I have some calls to make." Her father grimaced then left the room.

"Poor Camillo, getting all caught up in the middle of that," she said. "All he could do was run once he found out, since he didn't have a green card."

"And Cindy didn't let him."

Emilie nodded.

Derrick walked closer to the bed. "Can I hold your hand? There are so many tubes...."

Emilie lifted her left hand, which had only the pulse counter on her finger. Derrick took the tiny hand and tucked it into his own the way he'd wanted to do so many times. "How are you?"

"Good. Considering," she said, "I broke two ribs and my arm."

"And what else?"

"Nothing. That's it. I lost a lot of blood. That was the dangerous part. I'm having a transfusion now." She pointed to the bag of blood hanging on a metal pole near the bed. "But no internal injuries. And trust me, my dad made them do every test known to man."

"So, you'll be able to ride…."

"In a few weeks, I'll be able to do everything. Even go to trials."

"But the horses," Derrick said. "They won't test out because of the drugs. And all your wins this season, you'll have to forfeit them."

"You're right. Duchess and Marco won't test out," she said. "But Chelsea will. She was new this fall. I never let Cindy do the treatments on her."

"Beautiful Chelsea." Derrick pulled the chair to her bedside and reached over again for her hand. He turned her palm up and planted a kiss on it, then pressed it to his cheek.

Emilie smiled. "So, I think you had some things to tell me."

"I think *you* had some things to tell *me*," he said.

"I have your peace now, Derrick," she said. "I finally understand that God's love is not varying according to our circumstances. That it's constant."

"You have no idea how happy that makes me, Emilie." Derrick's throat closed with emotion.

"So, what about you?"

Derrick nodded. "I'm going back to school. I have enough money to finish up."

Her smile faded. "I know you need to do that… but I thought maybe—"

"Let me finish," he said. She had no idea how nervous he was. "I'm going to start a clinic for rescued horses with my uncle. Well, the clinic will be mine but I'm going to put it on some of his land and pay him off over time. Near this land is a home for troubled teens and I'm going to start a work program for them at my ranch. It will be my mission field."

"That's great, Derrick. You'll be great at that." He noticed some moisture gathering in her eyes.

He nodded. Could he tell her? What was the point? Her father didn't approve. Even in the stable when she said she'd turned to Christ, he knew it was still impossible. But at that moment, he'd also known that his love for her was too deep, too real, too important for him to ignore. He had to tell her how he felt. Then the decision would be hers. Derrick squeezed her hand, feeling the warmth of her fingers against his. "There's more, too...."

Emilie swallowed hard, not sure she wanted to hear the rest. Derrick was leaving. She would try to be supportive for him. He was doing what God had called him to. That should make her happy, right?

"I'm not rich," he continued. "I won't ever be able to offer you anything like what you're used to having. But I can't—"

Emilie scrunched up her nose and wiped her cheeks. "What are you talking about?"

Derrick dropped his head. "I'm trying to say that I love you."

"What?" Could it be true? That he felt what she did? Her heart was ready to burst at the thought.

Derrick lifted his head and looked her right in the eye. "I love you, Emilie Gill. So much. So deeply. I've never felt about any woman the way I feel about you."

Her eyes blinked rapidly. Her mouth was frozen. Her heart afraid to believe his words and wanting to all the same.

"Emilie, say something."

"Well…I don't understand. If you love me, then why are you leaving?"

"I'm not leaving *you*," he said with a smile. "I'm just leaving the stable. You, I want to keep seeing."

Emilie smiled, the tears flowing hard now. "I'd like that."

"Me, too." He leaned over and kissed her forehead.

But he wasn't smiling. There was still something unsettled in Derrick's expression, easily detected since he was rarely unsettled and couldn't hide it. "What else? There's something else…."

Derrick sighed. "Two things. Your father doesn't approve. And I feel like I'm asking you to give up an awful lot."

Emilie smiled. "I wouldn't think of being with you as giving anything up. And as for my father, he wants me to be happy."

"Then he and I want the very same thing," Derrick said.

Emilie sucked in a breath and began to cry.

"Don't cry, Emilie." He turned her palm up and pressed a kiss to it then pressed it to his cheek.

"I know. I'm just so happy," she said, tears streaming from her eyes. She pulled his face toward her. "Remember when I said I couldn't feel God's love? Well, I do now. Every time I look at you. I feel it. I love you, Derrick Randall."

Derrick leaned in and gave her a long, soft kiss.

TWENTY-FIVE

Three months later
The U.S. Olympic Jumper Team Trials,
Wellington, Florida.

Through a pair of high-powered binoculars, Derrick watched Emilie prepare for the final trial course. Ten days of riding in the Florida sun had covered her nose with freckles; she couldn't have looked more adorable.

He disliked cheering her on from the stands, but his coming was a surprise that Peter had asked him not to reveal until after her final ride. Emilie believed he was still at school. She also didn't know that Mrs. Kecksin had driven her RV down with a load of Emilie's friends and kids from the stable.

Derrick sat with Max, Karin and Mr. Gill. For hours, they watched over forty horse and rider combinations compete for only four Olympic jumper team spots. Going into the final round, Emilie and Chelsea held fifth place with an accumulation of ten faults over the course of the week. If she stayed in fifth, she would be asked to train for the summer as a substitute, but only the top four riders would travel to the Summer Games in September. Today, if she rode well and some other riders moved down, she might secure a higher ranking and make one of the top four spots.

Derrick felt excited for her, but the last two weeks had been difficult. She'd hardly had time to talk to him and he'd missed her like crazy. It didn't seem right that another groom was helping instead of him. He was more than anxious to go down and join her after that final ride.

"So what do you think about the course?" Mr. Gill asked.

"It's a tough one. Not very forgiving. She won't be able to ride fast and Chelsea likes speed." He shrugged his shoulders. "To move up she needs to ride clean and no one has done it today. Not even Leslie Raney."

"Emilie will," her father said. "I can feel it. So, Derrick, my daughter says you started building your clinic?"

"Yes, sir. Broke ground last week and I take my veterinary boards in the fall. If all goes well, I hope to open the clinic doors by the first of the year."

"I hope my daughter will like Tennessee," he mumbled.

Derrick lowered the binoculars and turned his head. Emilie's father had a strange look on his face.

"I—I—uh…" Derrick felt his pulse spike. "I haven't actually discussed that with Emilie. I—uh—"

"Well, when were you thinking of discussing it?" Mr. Gill asked.

"Sir?" Derrick swallowed hard. Ever since the hospital, Emilie's father had been okay with them dating, but Derrick hadn't had the guts to ask him about marriage.

"Preston. My name is Preston. So, are we planning a wedding soon? I need time to schedule these things, you know."

"I—I hardly know what to say." Derrick tried to use Mr. Gill's name, but he couldn't get the word off his tongue. "I haven't asked her yet. I don't know what she'll say."

"Miss Emilie Gill riding Chelsea's Danger," the deep voice announced over the loudspeaker.

"Not ever gonna find out if you don't ask." Max laughed from the row behind, then slapped him on the back.

Derrick didn't respond. Without budging a muscle, he watched Emilie ride the course, holding his breath, counting her strides, thinking through every movement, every turn, every touch of the hand and leg. What a thing of beauty she was on the back of that horse, guiding the young mare with total calm and confidence. The awe sent a shiver through him.

She approached the triple combination. It was the jump that had grabbed every rider.

"Do that big release, Emilie. Do it," he whispered.

Emilie folded and reached up to Chelsea's atlas, placing her hands just behind the horse's ears. The mare tucked gracefully over the jumps, her legs not even close to the top rails.

"She did it," Karin squealed. "She did it!"

The crowd responded by getting to their feet for the final line, everyone wanting to see if Emilie would be the first rider to make it through the course without a fault.

Derrick checked the time. Four seconds left. She needed to press through that last jump.

Emilie didn't look rushed as she led Chelsea to the finishing wall. Derrick ran a nervous hand through his hair as he watched the pair tuck together over the final obstacle. No rails. No faults. No time penalty.

The crowd erupted with applause as she crossed the time line. Emilie's family jumped up and down and hugged one another over her success. Derrick started pushing his way to the aisle. He couldn't wait to see Emilie any longer. But before he darted down the stairs, he turned back and took Mr. Gill's hand.

"Was that your consent, Mr. Gill?" he asked.

"Preston. I told you to call me Preston," he said with a nod. "And it was."

"Thank you."

"Do you even have a ring?" Max yelled at him.

Derrick gave his buddy a sly grin and hustled

down the stairs toward the park of trailers, trainers, horses and riders. His heart beating so fast his head swam.

"Congratulations on your placement," the sports announcer said on live television. "But we're all curious about the scandal caused by your former veterinarian. How long do you think she was doping your horses?"

Emilie removed her helmet and looked at the announcer. She was not pleased he had brought this up, but she'd already gotten a lot of practice answering this question. "There was evidence that she had done so for over a year. But not Chelsea. She never worked on Chelsea."

"Well, good luck to you and congratulations on representing the United States in the Summer Games."

She nodded to the announcer and moved off, looking around for Mr. Winslow. Her pulse still elevated, her body almost shaking in disbelief over her placement on the team. It was wonderful—what she had worked for and wanted for so long. But she wasn't as thrilled as she might have been. She was missing Derrick and making the team meant she'd be missing him even more in the upcoming months.

She continued searching through the crowd of people. Where was that trainer? She owed him an enormous hug. She searched the mass of people standing at the gates, which led to the trailers. No

Mr. Winslow. She shrugged, pulled off her gloves and walked on, every other person stopping to shake her hand and congratulate her.

"Congratulations, little rider."

Emilie stopped fast. A thrill deeper than any she'd ever known filled her every sense.

"Derrick." She spun around, dropped her helmet and gloves and leapt into his arms. "I'm so glad you're here. I missed you."

"And I missed you." He gave her a long kiss that turned her toes up then put her back on the ground. "I can't stay. I don't have a groom's pass. I had to take Peter's trainer card. But I'll see you tonight, okay?"

"Of course. I wish it were tonight already," she said.

"Me, too. Oh, and wave to everyone from the stable." He pointed to a group of people waving wildly at her from the stands.

"Oh my. That's Mrs. Kecksin and Susan and Bren and Megan and Deirdre and everyone… How did they all—"

"Mrs. Kecksin brought them all down. She's been planning the surprise for a long time."

"That's so sweet," she said. "Did you come with them?"

He nodded. "But I was hoping to get a ride back with you."

"You'd better." She threw her arms around him again.

"Peter wants back in. I'll see you soon." He kissed her cheek, looked hesitantly at her then started to walk back to the gate.

"Wait, Derrick. Don't go." She ran to him, closing in the distance between them.

He turned around and cradled her face with his hands. "What? I'll be right there with your family."

"I know but…" How could she tell him how she felt and be sure he would understand?

"Emilie, what's wrong? You just made the Olympic team. Why do you look so sad?"

"Okay." She grabbed his hands and held them tight. "Here's the thing. I like the new groom and all. She's very…competent. But for the Olympics, I was really hoping you might…"

"Be your groom?" he asked.

She nodded, her heart pounding, so afraid he had to say no because of all his plans.

"Well, that depends on how you answer this." Derrick slipped his hand from hers and pulled something from his pocket. He held his fist out in front of her and slowly revealed what lay in the center of his palm. A diamond ring, sparkling in the afternoon sun. He held it in front of her, his hand trembling a little. "Emilie Gill, would you be my bride?"

Unable to speak, she nodded. And tremors of joy waved down her spine as she slipped her finger into the ring. Images of her future flashed through her mind. She liked what she saw.

"What are you thinking, tiny rider?" he asked.

"I'm thinking that being announced as Emilie Randall will sound lovely when I'm entering the Olympic ring." She leaned up on her toes and gave her forever groom a kiss.

* * * * *

Dear Reader,

I'm so glad you decided to read my second Love Inspired Suspense novel, SABOTAGE. I hope you enjoyed the tale of Emilie and Derrick. Since horses have been a passion of mine for many years, I had great fun creating a story that unfolded in and around a stable. (Please note, however, that I did take several fictional liberties with the equine world. For example, there is no Winter Grand Prix Series in the state of Virginia.)

I thought of this story a few years ago, while reading a book about a husband and wife team who developed a ministry to abused children through a horse rescue ranch. Their place is located in Bend, Oregon, and has touched thousands of children and their parents. Their story truly inspired me and brought to heart the simple truth that we don't change people, God does and He does so through relationships.

Many blessings to you and yours,

Kit Wilkinson

QUESTIONS FOR DISCUSSION

1. Regardless of Emilie's faith, her struggles are universal—for example, accepting the unexpected/senseless death of a loved one. What in your life has made you question the sense of the universe? How did you work through it?

2. Derrick has great faith in God and great love for those around him, but he doesn't have a lot of direction. Have you ever known a "Derrick"? Did you envy or question his/her peace as Emilie does? Why or why not?

3. What is your favorite scene in the novel? Why?

4. Emilie wants love and approval from her father, who is emotionally unavailable to her. But as the story progresses, she starts to realize that's not what is really missing in her life. How do you think the changes in Emilie will affect her? Her relationship with her father? Her desire to be the best?

5. There's no question that Olympic athletes possess a drive that few of us can understand, but they forsake a lot to achieve their dreams and goals. Have you ever wanted something like

Emilie wants the Olympics? What things did you have to give up? Was it worth it?

6. Which character in the story do you relate to most? Why?

7. The relationship between horse and rider is strange and delicate. A horse can't usually see what's on the other side of a jump. He must trust the rider. The rider, on the other hand, is the weaker of the two and in that sense must have faith in his horse. In what ways does this relationship parallel our relationship with God and in what ways does it not?

8. Hebrews 11:1 says, "Faith is being sure of what we hope for and certain of what we cannot see." Explain how this verse gets to the crux of what is keeping Emilie from a relationship with God. What does the verse mean to you and your life?

9. What part of the equestrian world brought out in this novel did you find interesting? Why?

10. Mr. Winslow is the one and only character in the story who, basically, has no flaws. What does he represent to the story? To Emilie? To Derrick? Why is it important that he be a part of the story?

11. Karin (and Max) has a small role in the story but it's easy to tell that she has a lot of influence over Emilie. How is this evident? Why do you think Emilie doesn't turn to her more for comfort? Why go to Mr. Winslow instead?

12. What will happen to Mr. Gill? Will he ever slow down? Find love again? Find faith and joy? Why or why not?

HEARTWARMING INSPIRATIONAL ROMANCE

Contemporary,
inspirational romances
with Christian characters
facing the challenges
of life and love
in today's world.

**NOW AVAILABLE IN REGULAR
AND LARGER-PRINT FORMATS.**

Steeple
Hill®

For exciting stories that reflect traditional values,
visit:
www.SteepleHill.com